Petal Pushers

Too Many Blooms

Petal Pushers
Too Many Blooms

a novel by
Catherine R. Daly

SCHOLASTIC INC.

For the lovely, talented, and very patient Aimee.

With special thanks to Abby and Debra,
gratitude to my pals Lisa P. and Kiki,
and a big bouquet of roses to florist extraordinaire
Barbara Sunmark.

ISBN 978-1-338-16644-6

10 9 8 7 6 5 4 3 2 1   17 18 19 20 21

Printed in the U.S.A.   23
This edition first printing 2017

Book design by Yaffa Jaskoll

Chapter One

I waved good-bye to my best friend, Becky Davis, watching until she turned right at the end of the street. Then I took a deep breath and headed up the steps to my house. It had been a long week at school, but now it was Friday afternoon, and time to enjoy the weekend. I opened the front door, walked inside —

And immediately tripped over a pile of toys and shoes in the entrance hall.

Sprawled on my stomach, face-to-face with a chewed-up rubber chicken that still had dog drool on it, I sighed.

"Welcome home," I grumbled as I got to my feet.

I wondered, as I always did, if I was the only person in my house who didn't think that "organization" was a dirty word. I'm the oldest of four sisters, but sometimes I think my *parents* are actually the messiest members of the family!

1

I hung my coat in the closet and set my backpack by the stairs. Then I closed my eyes and inhaled. Mmm . . . was that roast chicken? My stomach rumbled. My mom is a great cook, but ever since my littlest sister Poppy started kindergarten, Mom's had more time on her hands. One of the results is that she's become a little too creative in the kitchen. Way too much glazed this and encrusted that for my taste. So plain old roast chicken sounded amazingly good to me. I made a silent wish that there wouldn't be anything weird like prunes, or even worse, oysters, in the stuffing. I made another for mashed potatoes. With gravy.

I could hear voices and music coming from the kitchen and I headed over to find Mom, Poppy, and one of my ten-year-old sisters, Aster, sitting at the old wooden table. Poppy was giving Mom a makeover so Mom's light brown hair — the exact same color as mine — was in three pig-tails, and one eyelid was purple and the other bright green. *Understated, yet elegant,* I thought. Aster sat across from them, peeling potatoes. She looked like a little witch in a black dress with black-and-white-striped tights and black boots with pointy toes. She gave me a nod. Aster is a girl of few words. She makes each one count.

Mom smiled when she saw me. Unfortunately, this was just as Poppy was applying bright red lipstick, so it ended up all over Mom's teeth. I tried not to laugh, but Mom looked like a vampire with terrible fashion sense.

"Hi, sweetie!" Mom said. "How was your day?"

"So-so," I replied, giving my tights a quick tug. That morning, I'd been so excited to wear a brand-new outfit, one I had bought with my own money: a cute, stripey sweater, a corduroy skirt with side zippers, and knee-high brown leather boots. I was halfway to school when I realized that my tights were slowly but surely inching their way down. I had put on tights that belonged to my other sister, Rose! (My dad does the laundry in our house, and he can never remember whose tights are whose.) There are few things in life more annoying than saggy, too-small tights. You have to yank on them all day long. Step. Yank. Step. Yank. It's enough to drive you insane.

It didn't help matters that my arch-nemesis, Ashley Edwards, called attention to my humiliating situation. "What's the matter, Del?" she had shouted from her locker, tossing her blonde hair over one shoulder. "Do you have ants in your pants or something?" Practically every seventh grader in the hallway had turned to stare — and laugh.

Then, in gym class, I'd been paired up with Rodney Franklin, the boy with the sweaty hands. Now, this wouldn't have been so bad if we were playing tetherball or anything else that didn't require constant hand-holding. But we were square dancing, a "unit" we'd apparently be doing all month. (Don't get me started on *that*.)

"Don't look so sad, Del," Poppy said earnestly. "Gran and Gramps are coming over tonight!"

I nodded, my spirits lifting. My grandparents come over every Friday night for dinner. We have make-your-own ice-cream sundaes for dessert and watch a movie. This week it was going to be *The Princess Bride*. Mom said it was one of her favorites. I couldn't wait.

"Aster, now it's time for *your* makeover!" Poppy announced, her golden curls bouncing.

"No," replied Aster, placing a peeled potato into a metal bowl next to her.

"Please, please, please, please, please," Poppy whined, clutching a large blush brush in her hand.

I leaned against the kitchen counter, wishing that I had stopped by the flower shop first instead of coming straight home. Gran and Gramps, along with Gran's big sister, my great-aunt Lily, own the only flower store in Elwood Falls, the small New Hampshire town where I live. The store is called Flowers on Fairfield, and it has been "Serving Your Floral Needs Since 1912." And Flowers on Fairfield has been in my mom's family since then.

As Gramps always tells me, "Flowers are in your blood." It's true. I can't remember a time when I haven't been in love with flowers. Not just the way they look and smell, which are both incredible, but the feeling of excitement you get when you open up a fresh delivery. And the look on a customer's face when they're presented with a perfectly put-together arrangement. Ever since I was little, I'd spent time at the store, helping out. But last year Gran and Gramps offered me an official job, paid and everything. I work on Saturdays, unpacking boxes of sweetheart roses, arranging gladioli in the refrigerated display case, and taking orders for birthday bouquets over the phone. It might not sound like much, but it's my absolute favorite place in the world to be.

And best of all — it's always neat and quiet. No piles of bills gathering dust. No broken toys, mismatched socks, and dirty dishes. No mountains of laundry waiting to be folded. And no annoying little sisters.

Just then the kitchen door opened and Dad's head popped in. His glasses fogged up from the sudden warmth.

"Introducing Rose Natalia Bloom!" he announced. "Otherwise known as *Bye Bye Birdie*'s Kim MacAfee!"

We all clapped as my sister walked into the room, her face flushed with excitement.

"Congratulations!" said Mom. "I'm so proud of you."

"It's a really fun role," Rose said, shrugging out of her coat. She let it drop to the floor and took center stage. As she launched into a song called "How Lovely To Be a Woman," I glanced at Aster, who watched Rose with a half smile on her face.

Aster and Rose are twins, but they could not possibly be more different. Their bedroom always makes me laugh — it's half pink (Rose's side) and half black (Aster's). Rose has wavy, blonde hair, blue eyes, and these all-American looks that could come straight from a Crewcuts catalog. She wears pastel cardigans, is president of the fifth-grade Drama Club, and has tons of friends. Pale Aster wears torn tights held together with safety pins, reads Edgar Allan Poe for fun, writes dark poetry, and has exactly one friend — a boy who seems to talk as little as she does. Still, my sisters are closer than close. Go figure.

I realized that Rose had finished her song and was looking at me expectantly. "Nice job, Rose," I said. I decided not to tell her about the tights mix-up. You never know when she's going to get overly dramatic about something. Goes with the territory, I guess.

"Thanks, Delphinium," she said with a grin.

Yes, Del is short for Delphinium. Not for Della or Delia, or anything else that's easy to pronounce. Most people don't call me by full name, thank goodness.

It's family tradition on my mom's side that all the girls are named after flowers. My mom's name is Daisy, which is about as cute as a name can get. And Gran is Iris, old fashioned, but still pretty. Great-aunt Lily has the nicest name of all, I think, though her grumpiness doesn't exactly match the loveliness of a lily. Rose is (usually) well suited to her cheery name. Aster has it hard sometimes, I guess. Poppy is a sweet name, though it does get an odd look now and then. But nothing beats Delphinium. Think about it. How many Delphiniums have you met?

Actually, delphiniums are really nice. They're delicate

and pretty. The bluish-purple flowers look like little bells. I like them a lot. My mom keeps reminding me that her favorite flower is the ranunculus. So when you think about it, I got off easy.

As Rose told Mom more about the play, Dad plopped down next to Aster. He picked up a short potato peel and put it under his nose like a mustache. My dad is a total goofball. Mom calls him the world's handsomest geek (with love, of course).

"And how was your day, my little Wednesday Addams?" he asked.

Aster gave Dad a small smile. She loves being compared to the dour Addams Family daughter. "Okay," she said. "I . . ."

I sniffed the air. I normally try not to interrupt Aster, since she speaks so infrequently. But I had to. "Do you smell something . . . burning?" I asked.

In an instant, Mom jumped up, threw on some oven mitts, and opened the oven door. Smoke billowed out and the smoke alarm began to wail. You know that sound. It feels like your head is about to split open. Buster, our Boston terrier, raced in and started barking. Dad grabbed the stepladder and climbed up to disconnect the alarm.

Mom sat at the table, her head in her oven-mitted hands. A blackened carcass sat on top of the stove.

"Roast chicken?" Rose asked. Mom nodded sadly. Everyone groaned.

"Anyone in the mood for Chinese?" I asked, already reaching for the phone.

"Great idea, Del!" called Dad from the stepladder. "Get an extra order of spare ribs this time. You know how much Aster loves them."

"She ate ten last time!" cried Poppy. "I counted!"

"Eight," Aster replied.

I dialed the number. I knew it by heart. Not to say that dinner got ruined often, but, well, I knew the number by heart is all I'm saying.

"Jade Mountain, how can I help you?" a woman's voice said.

"I'd like to place an order for pickup," I said. "I'll take two . . . no, make that three orders of spare ribs. Eight egg rolls. One large egg drop soup. Two orders of General Tso's chicken. One sizzling garlic shrimp. One order of Moo Goo Gai Pan. And . . ."

"Extra duck sauce, please!" everyone shouted.

9

"Extra duck sauce, please," I finished. I gave her my name and hung up.

"Fifteen minutes," I said. Dad offered to pick it up and Poppy insisted on going along with him. Rose and Aster disappeared up to their room, and I reminded Mom that we needed to clean up. I swear, sometimes I can't help feeling like *I'm* the grown-up.

Mom threw the big pile of shoes and toys into the hall closet while I tackled the bathroom, making sure we had guest towels and toilet paper. Oh, and I fished a flock of butterfly hair clips out of the toilet. The usual.

"Well, I guess we're ready," said Mom.

I stifled a laugh. "Not totally ready," I told her.

Mom looked puzzled.

I pointed to her head. "It's an interesting look," I said. "But a little bold for a family dinner?"

Mom's hand flew to her face and she started to laugh. "Maybe I'll tone down the makeup, huh?" she asked.

I had just finished setting the dining room table when Dad and Poppy returned. "Speedy delivery!" said Dad as he and Poppy unloaded the containers onto the kitchen counter. Aster, who had run downstairs as soon as she heard the car in the driveway, was eyeing the red-and-white bags of ribs hungrily. (Funny how she had managed to hear that, but she and Rose hadn't heard me calling them to help set up . . .)

"Don't even think about it," I told her.

She made a face.

The doorbell rang. "Gran and Gramps are here!" Poppy exclaimed. She barreled toward the door, flung it open, and threw her arms around Gran's legs.

"Now, Poppy, let them in first," said Dad.

My grandparents stepped inside, red-cheeked from their brisk walk in the cold air. Gran knelt down to give Poppy a big kiss, and then Gramps swung her in the air. "Again! Again!" she cried.

Rose and Aster kissed Gran while they both tried to grab the ice-cream bag from her mittened hand. Rose won.

"What kind?" Aster asked Gran.

"Peanut butter brickle," she replied. She and Gramps were in charge of the ice cream for our sundaes. They brought a different flavor every week.

"My favorite!" Aster and Rose cried at the same time.

I elbowed my way past my sisters and gave Gran a big

hug. I could feel the cold still lingering on her down coat. "How were things at the store?" I asked.

"Just fine, sweetheart," she said vaguely. She gave me a small smile, then looked away quickly.

"Is everything okay?" I asked her worriedly.

"Of course," she replied, then busied herself removing her coat and scarf.

I turned to Gramps and breathed in. "Gardenias," I said.

"Correct as usual, Del," he said. "We got a big shipment in today."

Dad stepped forward to take their coats. "Well, hello there, Professor Bloom!" Gramps said with a grin. That's what he almost always calls my dad, who teaches English literature at the local college. When my mom told her parents she had met a man named Benjamin Bloom, they thought she was joking. But she wasn't, and a year later she became Mrs. Daisy Bloom. My grandparents still get a laugh out of it.

We all filed into the dining room, which had a slight chill from the airing out we'd had to give the kitchen. But instead of charred food, all you could smell now was sweet-and-spicy chicken and the rich aroma of the ribs.

Mom had lit some long taper candles and dimmed the lights, giving the room a homey glow.

"I burned dinner," Mom admitted cheerfully.

Gran gave Mom a sympathetic smile. "If I had a nickel for every time I did that . . ." she said ruefully.

Gramps laughed. "We'd be richer than the Rockefellers!" he joked. "Is that General Tso's chicken I smell?"

"Bingo!" said Poppy. "And I picked it up with Daddy!" she added proudly.

We all sat around the table and started grabbing containers and helping ourselves. I poured myself a bowl of egg drop soup, rich and creamy. As I dropped in some crispy chow mein noodles, I stole a glance at Gran. Something wasn't right. She was nervously tapping her fingers on her water glass. Gramps reached over and patted her hand reassuringly. I frowned — what could be wrong?

Nah, I must be imagining things, I decided. I picked up my spoon and started to eat my soup.

We had all been pretty silent as we loaded our plates. Then, as is usually the case in my house, everyone started talking at once.

"Ribs, please," Aster said to Dad.

"Guess who got the lead in the school play!" Rose exclaimed.

"I wish I was a dolphin," said Poppy wistfully.

"Does it still smell like smoke?" Mom wondered.

"We had the most fascinating discussion on *The Canterbury Tales* today . . ." said Dad.

Everyone laughed. "Rose, you go first," Dad said.

Gramps cleared his throat. "Actually, maybe *I* should go first," he said gravely. "Gran and I have an announcement to make."

That shut everyone up immediately. We all stopped chewing and stared. Even Poppy looked serious.

"Announcement?" said Mom uncertainly.

"Is something wrong?" I asked, my voice rising. My heart started to pound double-time.

"No, it's all good news," said Gran. But she sure didn't look too happy. She took a deep breath and began. "We've thought about it long and hard. It was a terribly difficult decision to make, but . . ." her voice trailed off.

"But what?" I managed to choke out.

"Yes, what?" Rose cried.

Gramps took a deep breath. "We've been thinking about retiring," he said. "And —"

"Wait . . . what?" I interrupted, so shocked I dropped my spoon. It fell into the bowl with a clatter, splashing my new sweater with egg drop soup. But I hardly even noticed.

Gramps held up a hand and continued. "Yes, we are thinking about retiring, but we're not quite ready to hand over the reins of the store for good. So we have an idea we'd like to run by you."

We all leaned forward to hear. I placed my hands on my stomach, which was tied up in knots.

Gramps turned to my parents. "We'd like the two of you to take over the store for three months. We're going to take an extended trip to Florida."

"Florida?" said Poppy. "Like . . . Disney World?"

"Florida?" I said. "But that's so far away!"

Gran turned to me, her eyes shining. "It's only a short plane ride," she said. "And it's an opportunity we just can't refuse. Our friends the Isaacs are going on a long trip to Italy and they've asked us if we'd like to house-sit. Three months in Key West, rent free, can you believe it?"

I tried to swallow, but I had a huge lump in my throat. I reached for my water glass.

"Did you know that the sunsets down there are so beautiful that people actually applaud for them?" Gran asked.

"Wow," said Poppy, clapping her hands.

Now that the news was out, Gran had relaxed. Her cheeks were bright pink. She looked so pretty and excited in the candlelight, her curly white hair like a halo around her head.

"We're going to grill every night," she continued, "and go sailing. And the snorkeling there is phenomenal! You can see nurse sharks and turtles and all kinds of fish . . ."

Rose was frowning. *Yes!* I thought. *She knows what a ridiculous idea this is, and she's going to say something.* But then she smiled. "Well, Dad will just have to film *Bye Bye Birdie* so you can see it," she said. "But otherwise it sounds like a great idea to me."

I rolled my eyes. Of course Rose had one thing on her mind — theater!

I turned to Aster. She was sensitive. Surely *she*

understood how wrong this was. But — no. "I've always wanted to go to the Everglades," she said quietly.

Seriously?

"Good!" said Gramps with a grin. He turned back to Mom and Dad. "So we'll leave you two in charge of the store on a trial basis. And if you can make a go of it, we just may leave Flowers on Fairfield in your hands. Permanently."

I looked over at my parents. They sat in silence, blinking in confusion.

Which was exactly how I felt. Gran and Gramps were leaving for three months? Possibly for good? And leaving the store in my parents' hands? Dad didn't know a thing about flowers. Plus, he had a full-time job. Mom hadn't worked in the flower shop since she was in high school. I was the only one who knew anything about the store. Was I supposed to quit school and work there full-time? What were my grandparents thinking?

To my utter shock and amazement, a grin spread over my mother's face. "What a great idea!" she cried. "We'll miss you terribly, of course," she added. "But now that Poppy's in school, I've been thinking about going back to work."

Dad smiled at Mom. "It's true," he said. "We were just talking about it last night. This couldn't come at a better time."

Gran exhaled loudly. "Well, that's a relief," she said.

"Now that that's settled," said Gramps, "please pass the ribs."

Everyone else chattered away as they finished eating. Some even took second helpings. Aster ate nine ribs. (I counted.) But I had lost my appetite.

"Hey!" Dad said. "Let's go into my office and look up Key West on the Internet. If you know the address, we can even look up your new house on Google Maps."

"Great idea!" said Gran. Everyone stood up and headed out to Dad's study. I stayed behind, staring at the sputtering candles. Then I noticed the pile of fortune cookies on the table.

I grabbed one, tore off the wrapper, and cracked it open.

AT THE WORST OF TIMES YOU MUST SUMMON YOUR OPTIMISM, it read.

Who was I to question the wisdom of the fortune cookie? I blew out the candles, pasted a big fake smile on my face, and went to join my family.

Chapter Two

I knelt in the front window of the flower shop, replacing last week's display with some cheerful lilacs and daffodils. It sure didn't feel like it, but spring was on its way. We technically have four seasons in New England, but sometimes it feels like winter for half the year.

As I adjusted the fragrant yellow and purple flowers, I watched Gran and Gramps bustling around as if they hadn't dropped the biggest bombshell in the world last night.

This was usually my favorite time of the day in the store. The three of us working together in companionable silence, just before the phone started ringing and customers started coming in. I sighed. I loved the store so much — the creaky wooden floors and creamy white walls, the row of pretty glass vases that I dusted each week. The buckets that held ready-made bouquets for walk-in customers. Even the rattle of the old flower cooler was gentle and calming. The only thing that ever changed was the year on the floral supply calendar behind the cash register.

Of course, things get busy around Mother's Day, and the days leading up to February 14 are always crazy. We had recently finished up with Easter, with its ton of basket bouquets. And don't get me started on prom season. But most days Gran could be found quietly arranging flowers while Gramps balanced the books or paid bills. Bliss.

Not for long, Delphinium Bloom, I thought morosely. *Not for long.*

"Great work, Del," said Gran, broom in hand. I turned to her, that same fake smile still plastered on my face. She cocked her head at me. "You've been awfully quiet. How are you feeling about the big news?"

"Okay," I lied. "I'm happy for you and Gramps." Although it wasn't true, I would at least act like it was. Even if it killed me.

As my grandparents went out back to put some boxes in the recycling bin, there was the familiar

Ring-a-ling-ling! of the front door opening. The first customer of the day!

I looked up and smiled. "Welcome to . . ."

And stared into the scowling face of Aunt Lily.

"No need for that," she said brusquely, taking off her gloves, finger by finger. My dad calls Aunt Lily a throwback to another era. She always looks picture perfect, I have to admit. As usual, her white hair was in a sleek chignon and she was wearing a large hat. She's the only person I know who still uses hat pins.

Aunt Lily set her ancient, though pristine, alligator purse on the counter, watching me carefully, as if she were afraid I'd rifle through it. Actually, she had a point. Two years ago, Poppy had made off with her purse and ate an entire tube of Kiss Me Coral lipstick. We called poison control and everything. But my lipstick-eating days are long gone. Aunt Lily, however, did not look too sure about that.

"Where is that scatterbrained sister of mine?" she asked me.

I frowned. "Gran is in the back," I said as politely as possible through my gritted teeth. "Let me get her for you."

I get so mad whenever Aunt Lily makes comments about Gran, who tends to be a little scatterbrained, it's true. It's where my mom gets it from. Gran has been known to leave her cell phone in the freezer while putting away groceries (never a good idea). And Gramps likes to tell the story of when they first took over the store from Gran's parents and she accidentally sent a "Congratulations on the Good News!" arrangement to the funeral parlor and a "With Deepest Sympathy" to a new mom of twins. Yikes!

I found Gran and Gramps walking in the back door. "Aunt Lily is here," I announced.

Gran and Gramps exchanged a glance. "You don't think she already knows, do you?" asked Gramps. Gran shook her head, but she looked worried.

My mouth fell open. "You haven't told her yet?" I asked in disbelief.

"We were going to call her last night after we spoke to your parents," said Gramps with a grimace. "But in all the excitement, we forgot."

Gran wiped her hands on her flowered apron as she and Gramps headed to the front of the store. I followed close behind. I was filled with dread, but still I didn't want to miss a thing.

Aunt Lily gave Gran a tight smile. "Well, hello there, Iris," she said in a clipped tone. "I spoke with your daughter this morning, who informed me that she and Benjamin will be taking over the store while you two go gallivanting down to Florida." She narrowed her eyes. "Surely she must be mistaken?"

Gran opened her mouth, but nothing came out. Her big sister always makes her nervous. Even after all these years.

Gramps put his hands on Gran's shoulders. "Now Lily," he said. "We were going to tell you today. We just wanted to make sure that Daisy and Ben were on board first."

Aunt Lily put her hand to her forehead as if she'd felt a sharp and sudden pain. "And you expect me to agree to turn over the store to my lovely, though disorganized, niece?" She narrowed her eyes. "Are you forgetting I own one third of this business?"

Aunt Lily is part owner of the store, but she hasn't done any of the day-to-day business in years. She's way too busy, she says, with her charity work. "And her gossiping," Dad likes to say. Aunt Lily does always seem to have the inside scoop on everything going on around town. She gets all the news from her charity lady friends. (We call it the "Old Lady Mafia," though never in front of her, of course!)

But she's still involved in the store, and she usually seems to drop by at the worst possible times. It's like she has disaster radar or something.

Gran spoke up, her voice clear but shaky. "Lily, we've thought about this long and hard. We have an opportunity we can't pass up. It's only a trial run. And yes, I do think that Daisy and Ben will do a great job."

Aunt Lily turned to me and pursed her lips. "And do you agree, Delphinium?"

"I . . . um . . ." I looked wildly from Gran to Gramps to Aunt Lily. I can't help it — Aunt Lily scares me. And when I'm scared, I can't fib. It gets me in trouble all the time.

Suddenly, there was a rap on the glass door. We all spun around. A young woman was standing outside, waving frantically.

I stepped forward and opened the door. Whew! Saved by the customer. "Welcome to Flowers on Fairfield," I said to her in my most professional-sounding voice. "Can I help you?"

The woman looked to be in her midtwenties. Her long, blonde hair was pulled into a perfect ponytail, not a strand out of place. She had big, blue eyes and was wearing light pink lipstick. She was just so pretty and perfect looking, like a mannequin. And . . . I couldn't put my finger on it, but something about her seemed familiar.

Oddly enough, she had her hands in the air, as if she was afraid to touch anything. *Maybe she's one of those germ-phobic weirdos,* I thought.

"I just got a mani-pedi!" she exclaimed as she stepped inside. "Don't want to smudge my nails!" She smiled, flashing her straight, white teeth. I found myself nodding in sympathy and returning her grin, although I wasn't totally sure what she was talking about. Manny who?

"Oh, okay," I said.

"Would you be a sweetheart and put Louis on the floor?" she asked me.

"Louis?" I asked.

She looked at me like I had two heads. "Louis Vuitton?" she said, nodding toward the bag slung over her shoulder. That's when I noticed that there was a tiny, shivering dog poking its face out of her large purse. I reached inside and

25

picked up the dog, who instantly snarled and began yapping at me. As I placed the pet on the floor, I blinked. Was Louis wearing a tiny, black leather motorcycle jacket? Why, yes he was.

The customer looked around. "So this is it," she said with a sigh. "I was hoping it would be . . . fancier."

My mouth fell open. How rude! Luckily, Gran sensed my annoyance and stepped right in, putting on her most gracious smile. "How can we help you, dear?" she said.

"My name is Olivia Post," the woman said. She held out her left hand. A huge diamond sparkled on her ring finger. "I got engaged last night!" she gushed. "Five carats, cushion cut, can you believe it?"

We all oohed and ahhed although I don't know if any of us, except for Aunt Lily, knew exactly what "cushion cut" meant. "So," Olivia continued. "I wanted to have a spring wedding. May nineteenth!" She turned to me and said, "Saturday, of course!"

Gran smiled and nodded, but she looked distracted. I knew she was calculating how many weeks that would give us. Her widened eyes said it all — not many.

"And where will it be held?" Gran asked.

"At the Country Club," Olivia replied. She wrinkled her brow. "Of course," she added.

"Will it be a large wedding?" Gramps wanted to know.

"Oh, only a couple hundred guests," explained Olivia.

Gramps and I exchanged glances. That was huge by anyone's standards! In fact, the biggest wedding I had ever been to — for Dad's sister, my aunt Stacey — had had about fifty guests. Okay, I'll admit it. That was the *only* wedding I had ever been to.

"But I really want it to have an intimate feel," Olivia continued. "And it's got to be special. I don't know if I've mentioned this, but my fiancé is Todd Worthington." She paused meaningfully.

"Oh, of course," said Aunt Lily. She turned and gave us all a significant look.

We looked back at her blankly.

Aunt Lily glared at us. "The mayor's eldest son," she hissed, clearly disgusted by our ignorance.

We all nodded.

"There will be some very important people at the wedding," explained Olivia. "So I want a wedding like no one has ever been to before. I'm thinking ice sculptures, a couple of chocolate fountains, a sushi station . . . So the flowers, of course, have to be exquisite," she concluded.

Gran went behind the counter and hauled out the huge photo album filled with snapshots of all the weddings, parties, and events she and Gramps had done over the years. I loved flipping through that book during down time in the store. The fashions (High-necked lacy dresses that looked like nightgowns! Powder blue tuxes with ruffly shirts!) and the hairstyles (Huge pouffy updos! Shaggy hair and gigantic sideburns!) changed, but the flowers always looked beautiful.

Olivia held up her hand like a crossing guard telling cars to stop. "No thank you," she said. She spoke precisely, as if Gran were slightly slow and needed extra time to process her words. "My flowers need to be one of a kind. One. Of. A. Kind." She smiled sweetly.

Gran looked panicked. I knew what she was thinking. In two weeks she and Gramps were going to be snorkeling with the sea turtles. And Aunt Lily had rattled her. *Would my mom be able to handle this?* Slowly, Gran shook her head. "I don't know if this is a good time," she said. "You see, there's going to be a change in management . . ."

"Iris . . ." Aunt Lily's voice was sharp. She stared daggers at Gran.

"I'm sorry," said Gran, "but I just don't think there's enough time . . ." Her voice trailed off.

Olivia flipped a hand dismissively. "I'm sure the florist in Plymouth would be happy for my business if you can't handle it," she said.

"Iris," Aunt Lily said again.

I cleared my throat. "There's no problem at all," I heard myself saying. *Wait! Stop! Del!* my brain protested. But my mouth kept moving. "We will give you the wedding of your dreams. The most exquisite floral arrangements this town has ever seen!"

Everyone stared at me in shock. Except Olivia. She just smiled at me as if twelve-year-olds routinely took charge of planning weddings. "Excellent!" she said. "I'm off to try on dresses." She smiled. "I'll be back soon with a few friends to discuss themes." Checking her nails, she picked up Louis Vuitton and gave him a kiss on top of his head. Then she whipped out her cell phone and placed a call.

"Hello. I am interested in ordering six dozen white doves, spray painted pink," she said on her way out.

29

The door shut behind her. "Oh, Del, you were great!" cried Gran, giving me a squeeze. Then she stepped back and looked into my eyes. "Do you really think you can handle it?"

"No problem, Gran," I said. I stole a glance at Aunt Lily. She gave me a funny little head shake. *Is that a nod of approval?* I wondered. Then I realized who I was dealing with. *Nah, she probably just has a twitch.*

My heart was pounding. I leaned my head against the front door and breathed out, leaving a fog on the cool glass. I traced my initials. I could hardly believe it. I had just agreed to do the flowers for an impossible-to-please Bridezilla with unrealistic expectations. In a matter of weeks, no less.

My stomach sank. What had I gotten myself into?

Chapter Three

I focused on the goofy GOT ROSES? bumper sticker on Gran and Gramps's Buick, staring hard so my tears wouldn't fall. As the car pulled away, I stole a glance inside and saw Gran waving from the passenger seat while Gramps frantically pushed buttons on his brand-new GPS.

We all waved back until the car, packed to the gills with suitcases, fishing poles, and lawn chairs, became a tiny dot in the distance. Then I looked down at my red patent leather ballet flats, avoiding eye contact with the rest of my family. I *would not* cry.

This was really happening. Gran and Gramps were gone.

We stood in silence. Finally, Dad cleared his throat. "'Parting is such sweet sorrow,'" he said solemnly. "William Shakespeare."

Dad loves to quote authors. He says it's an occupational hazard, all those words popping into his head to describe every life event. It's sometimes interesting and sometimes annoying. Like a lot of things are, I guess.

Then Dad sighed. "I'd better get Poppy to kindergarten," he said, and gave my mom a hug and a kiss. "Good luck, Daisy Bloom," he added.

"Yeah, break a leg, Mom," said Rose. She never gives that theater thing a rest, I swear.

Mom, who has no problem crying in public, wiped her eyes with one of the colorful bandannas she always carries. This one was bright red, to match the big gerbera daisy on her T-shirt. She gave us a shaky smile — a combination of sad, nervous, and excited. Then she placed her hand on her stomach.

"Butterflies?" I asked. I knew she was nervous to open the store for the first time all by herself. But Dad had class that morning and couldn't be there.

She nodded. "It feels like the first day of school," she said, puffing out her cheeks and blowing out a stream of air. "And I'm the new girl," she added.

"You'll be great, Mom," I said. I didn't add *I hope*, although I certainly was thinking it.

Gran and Gramps had spent the past two weeks teaching Mom and Dad the day-to-day operations of a flower shop. How to take orders, how to put together floral arrangements, how to contact vendors, etc. I hoped my parents had been paying attention.

The semester was winding down, so Dad would be around to help — both with the store and with house chores. I'd still work Saturdays and pitch in after school if needed. Mom had suggested that Rose and Aster could also help, but I'd vetoed that idea. After all, I'd explained, *I* was the responsible Bloom sister, and I hadn't even officially been on staff until I was eleven. The twins could wait a year. It was only fair.

What I didn't mention to my family was that even in a year's time I didn't think my sisters would be ready. Besides, with my help, why did we need anyone else? They would just mess things up.

Poppy stepped up to Mom. "For luck," she said, handing her something.

"Oh, Poppy!" said Mom as the tears began to flow

again. "Thank you!" She held up Poppy's gift — a tiny, plastic windup dog that did flips. "I'll keep it on the counter where I can see it all day," she said.

Poppy looked very pleased.

After Mom hugged and kissed each of us (she has been known to give us kisses when we leave the living room to get a glass of water, I swear), Dad and Poppy took off for the elementary school. They were followed by Rose and Aster, who linked arms, their blonde and dark brown heads bent together. I felt a slight twinge of envy at their closeness. But then, I reminded myself, they had to share a room. Not so fun. Not to mention a birthday. Even worse.

I headed in the opposite direction toward my middle school, sticking my cold hands in my jacket pockets. I was so distracted that morning, I had left my hat and gloves at home. And now I was paying for it.

I arrived at school, walked up the granite steps, and pushed open the front door. It was still on the early side, so my shoes made hollow sounds as I walked down the empty hallway toward my locker. I breathed in the baby aspirin smell of the cleaning spray the janitor used. I love that sweet orangey aroma. If someone created a perfume called Freshly Cleaned Sarah Josepha Hale Middle School Hallway, I'd be first in line to buy it.

I came to a stop in front of my locker and opened it with a snap. I smiled. Neat as a pin, just the way I liked it. I hung my jacket and placed my books in the top section, in alphabetical order, of course: English, health, history, math, science, Spanish. I selected the books, notebooks, and folders I needed for my morning classes. I was about to swing the door closed with my hip when I had a thought: Spinach and Swiss cheese omelet for breakfast equals possible green stuff in teeth. Middle school suicide. I placed my books on the floor and checked myself out in the magnetic mirror I had stuck in the top of my locker. I smiled widely and spotted a largish piece of green in between my two front teeth. *Nice catch, Del!* I thought, relieved. I removed the piece of spinach and bared my teeth again. All clear.

"Dental hygiene is a very important part of my day, too," said a voice behind me.

Startled, I swung my head around, clocking it on the edge of the locker door. *Oof!* Clutching my forehead, I blinked at the person who had spoken. It was a boy. An unfamiliar boy. A very cute, unfamiliar boy. A very cute, unfamiliar boy who had just seen me picking my teeth! I stared at him.

"Hey," he said.

Though I wished the freshly polished floor would open and swallow me up, I found myself taking in his longish, sandy brown hair, lazy smile, even teeth, and piercing blue eyes. That's right, I said *piercing*.

"Hey," I managed to squeak out. And then, what did I do? I scooped up my books and took off down the hall.

Not one of my finer moments.

As I got farther down the hall, away from Mr. Dental Hygiene, I had to laugh at myself. Imagine me, Delphinium Bloom, getting all flustered by a boy. That just doesn't happen to me. Or to my best friend, Becky. We're not like some of the other girls in our grade who have a different crush every day, who doodle hearts and arrows in their notebooks when they should be taking notes in class.

Not, I must mention, that Becky and I are social misfits or anything. We may be serious about school, but we are fashionable. Becky is definitely the prettier of us two: she's tall and slim, with dark brown skin, brown eyes, and black curly hair that comes to her shoulders. But I'll admit that I can pass for cute, too. I have wavy light brown hair, hazel eyes, and pale skin that freckles in the summer.

Still, being distracted by boys has always seemed kind of . . . frivolous. So I was surprised that I felt like I was about to burst if I didn't tell Becky what had just happened.

When I reached the cafeteria table we sit at each morning, my heart sank. Becky, who sat across from our friend Heather Hanson, was studying from her Spanish flash cards, which meant she was having a quiz that day. Which also meant Becky would only want to converse in Spanish. I generally humor her, but today was not the day to be hampered by my less-than-stellar foreign-language skills.

"*Hola,*" said Becky. "*Siéntese.*"

I sat.

"Spanish quiz," Heather told me, flipping through the latest copy of *Us Weekly*.

Heather looks like a porcelain doll, with her heart-shaped face, corkscrew curls, and dimpled cheeks. She's tough, though, and doesn't think twice about telling you exactly what's on her mind, which always surprises people who are expecting a sweet girly girl.

"*¿Qué pasa?*" Becky asked, taking in my flushed cheeks. She picked up a carton of orange juice and took a swig.

Hmmm. I didn't know how to say *I was picking my teeth* in Spanish, but I decided I knew enough words to say, "I was stupid in front of a cute boy."

"*Era estupido antes de un*"— I searched my brain for the Spanish word for *handsome* —"*guano muchacho*," I finished triumphantly.

Becky promptly spat out her orange juice, showering her flash cards. And me.

"You were stupid in front of a poopy boy?" she told me when she could finally talk. "I guess you meant to say *guapo* instead of *guano*?"

"*Sí*," I admitted, my cheeks flaring again.

"Sorry, Del," she said, shaking her head, a huge grin on her face. "But you have to admit, that was really funny."

Heather put down her magazine and leaned forward eagerly. "So tell us about Señor Guapo!" she said.

All thoughts of studying went out the window as Becky, along with Heather, peppered me with questions, thankfully all in English. Before long, the whole embarrassing story was out.

Becky bit her lip. "Well, that's not *so* bad . . ." she said. Heather gave her a dubious look.

"What planet are you from?" I asked. "I picked my teeth *and* bumped my head. Maybe if I had some toilet paper stuck to my shoe, that would have made my humiliation complete." I quickly glanced down at my ballet flats. No trailing TP. Thank goodness.

"Yeah," said Heather. "That's about as bad as it gets!" She grinned, showing her matching dimples.

"Thanks, Heather," I said sarcastically. "As if today wasn't bad enough, having to say good-bye to Gran and Gramps."

Becky's face fell. "Oh, Del," she said. "That's right. I'm so sorry."

"And right this very moment Mom is opening the store by herself." I sighed. "I'm a little nervous."

"Don't obsess, Del," said Heather with a wave of her hand as she returned to her magazine. "She's a grown-up. She'll be fine."

But Becky gave me a sympathetic look. She knew how important the store was to me. And how worried I was that Mom wouldn't be able to handle it. I gave her a grateful smile back and checked my watch. Fifteen minutes to the first-period bell. I grabbed some money from my bag and walked up to the counter. It was definitely feeling like a hot-chocolate-with-whipped-cream kind of morning. The nice breakfast lady noticed my wan expression and smiled as she gave me an extra squirt of whipped cream. I was just about to take a big spoonful of creamy deliciousness when I felt a tap on my shoulder. Turning around, I nearly dropped my hot cocoa.

Just my luck. It was Ashley Edwards, flanked by her two handmaidens — I mean best friends — Sabrina Jones and Rachel Lebowitz. Sabrina and Rachel look almost exactly alike — only distinguishable by a slight difference in the shade of their straight brown hair and the fact that Sabrina says the word "like" like all the time.

Way back in preschool, Ashley and I were inseparable. But then we had what Becky and I like to call The Teletubby Incident. Ashley and I both showed up on Halloween dressed as Tinky Winky — you know, the tall, purple one. My costume was much better. (Ashley didn't even have the red purse — what was up with that?) And Ashley has never gotten over it. She apparently likes to be one of a kind, fashion-wise. Rumor has it that she texts her handmaidens her outfit choice every morning so there will be no inadvertent clothing cloning.

And talk about boy crazy. Ashley played spin the bottle at her fifth-grade birthday party. (And no, I wasn't there. But everyone talked about it for months.) Ashley is also spoiled rotten — she has all the latest clothes and accessories. Despite myself, I realized I was admiring her outfit that morning. Midnight blue crushed-velvet leggings, tall suede boots, and an off-the-shoulder crocheted sweater over a tank top. A cute beret completed the look. I once tried wearing a hat indoors and the whole time I walked through the halls thinking, *Look at me, I am wearing a hat.* I stuffed it into my backpack in third period. And that was the end of the Great Hat Experiment.

I am *so* not jealous of Ashley, though.

Okay, so maybe I'm a little bit jealous of her clothes, her Brazilian-straightened blonde hair, and her social life. So sue me.

"Hello, Ashley," I said coolly.

Ashley stared at me for a moment, then spoke. "My cousin tells me that she's considering letting your family do the flowers for her wedding," she said as if this had to be a mistake.

41

"Um, your cousin?" I said.

Ashley rolled her eyes. "Well, this is totally awk," she said to her friends. Ashley is always talking in shorthand. Terrif. Gorge. Fab. You get the picture. It is so totally obnox, as she would say. "Olivia Post?" She looked back at me. "Um, the biggest wedding of the year?"

Suddenly, it all made sense. No wonder Bridezilla had seemed so familiar. Of course, the two most spoiled rich girls I had ever met were related!

Ashley stepped closer to me. "This is the most important wedding this town has ever seen," she added, sounding just like Olivia had yesterday. She smiled. "And *I'm* going to be a junior bridesmaid!" Sabrina and Rachel oohed and ahhed as if they were hearing the news for the first time, which I was absolutely certain they were not. Ashley narrowed her eyes at me. "So do you think you can handle it, Delphinium? Hmmmm?"

"Don't you worry, Ashley," I said, as dignified as I could be. "Flowers on Fairfield has been serving your floral needs since 1912." I cringed as I said it. *Good one, Del,* I thought. *You sound like a brochure! A lame brochure.*

Ashley rolled her eyes. "Whatev." Her two handmaidens

nodded their heads. Then, in unison, they turned and flounced off.

"What a jerk!" I muttered under my breath, frustrated that I hadn't come up with anything good to say back to her. I never can. It annoys me so much.

I sighed. As if this big wedding without Gran and Gramps wasn't bad enough. Now I had the added pressure of my enemy watching over the whole thing. Yikes!

By the time I got back to the table, I was disappointed to see that the whipped cream had already dissolved into my hot chocolate. I gulped the cocoa down just before the bell rang. My friends and I gathered our books and headed to class.

Thankfully, my day ended up getting better. I got a tough answer right in math class. My teacher handed back our English papers, and I got an A-minus. And the cafeteria served pepperoni pizza at lunchtime. But I still couldn't stop thinking about the wedding. And Ashley. And Mom all alone in the flower store. What a recipe for disaster!

Finally, it was the last class of the day. Most of my friends think I am lucky because I have gym last period. That means I don't have to go back to class all sticky and sweaty. Which is good. But the bad part is that both Ashley Edwards and a bully named Bob Zimmer are in my class. Luckily, the two of them are paired together for square dancing. I'll take Rodney Franklin and his sweaty hands over mean Bob any day.

As always, we were sitting in rows on the uneven, wooden gym floor, waiting for class to begin. I glanced down at the world's most unattractive gym uniform. I know what you're thinking — gym uniforms are *supposed* to be ugly. There's practically a rule about that. But are your school colors yellow and purple? Didn't think so.

Mr. Rolando, my gym teacher, stood in front of us taking attendance. I was idly wondering which state Gran and Gramps were in by then. It was a long trip, and I hoped they wouldn't try to drive too far on their first day. I was startled back to reality when Mr. Rolando blew his whistle. I looked up. And there stood Señor Guapo, the cute boy from that morning.

Are you kidding me? I thought. Out of the corner of my eye I could see Ashley leaning forward with interest. For some reason, this totally irked me.

"Class, please welcome our new student, Hamilton

Baldwin," said Mr. Rolando. Everyone mumbled a half-hearted hello.

That was why I hadn't recognized him. New kid. I stared at the boy formerly known as Guapo. Despite my mortification, my next thought was: *He looks good in yellow and purple.* And let me tell you, that is not an easy feat.

Mr. Rolando consulted his attendance sheet. "And since . . . Rodney Franklin is out today, you can partner up with Delphinium Bloom," he told Hamilton in his booming gym teacher voice. "Del, will you raise your hand?"

My heart immediately started pounding like crazy. *Why me?* I thought. I waved my hand weakly at my new dance partner. Maybe he wouldn't recognize me in my uniform. It was my only hope.

Hamilton grinned as he walked over. He flopped to the ground beside me. "Dental Hygiene Girl!" he said. "What's up?"

I smiled despite myself. And my face, once again, turned hot.

"I didn't mean to startle you this morning," he said. "By the lockers," he added.

As if he had to explain!

"No problem," I said, studying his black Converse Hi-Tops. They were as long as surfboards, I swear. "So you're new?" I added lamely.

"Yeah, we just moved here. My mom, stepdad, and me." He frowned for a moment. "Hey, if I say something, do you promise not to get offended?"

I narrowed my eyes at him. "It depends," I said warily.

"I've gone to a couple of different schools in my life," he said, "and I can honestly tell you that I have never seen a gym uniform as ugly as this one. We all look like Easter eggs!"

I couldn't help myself. I snorted. Loudly. "You're right!"

Ashley, who was sitting directly across from me in the next row, leaned over. "Very ladylike, Del," she said, giving Hamilton a big smile.

To my delight, Hamilton ignored her. He leaned closer to me. "Who's that?" he whispered. "The captain of the manners police?"

I laughed like it was the funniest thing I had ever heard. Ashley gave me a dirty look.

As I searched for something witty, or at least not lame, to say to Hamilton, Mr. Rolando blew his whistle again, signaling the beginning of class. We were learning a new dance today. Mr. Rolando put his hands on his hips and began to demonstrate the steps. I had to give him credit, for a muscle-bound gym teacher, he was certainly light on his feet.

Then it was our turn. "Ladies to the gents' right," Mr. Rolando instructed.

"Yee-hah," I said weakly, and Hamilton chuckled.

As we formed our square, Hamilton said, "I have to warn you, I am totally uncoordinated when it comes to dancing."

"You couldn't be any worse than my regular partner," I said as the music started.

But I was wrong. Very wrong.

Hamilton was the most terrible square dancer ever. But he laughed every time he stepped on my feet. And so did I. When he accidentally bumped into me and I went flying into Ashley and Bob, and she said loudly, "As smooth as ever, Delphinium," I didn't even care. Very strange.

And the weirdest part of all? This time it was *my* hands that were sweaty.

Chapter Four

On the walk home, I finally thought of the perfect Ashley comeback. Just after she'd said, "So do you think you can handle it, Delphinium?" I should have held up my palm to her, smirked (a very important detail), and said, totally seriously, "Calm down, Tinky Winky."

Why do I always think of the perfect response about twenty-four hours after the fact? I hate it when that happens. Which is *always*.

I was about to head straight for my house, but I stopped. I knew I should give Mom a break and not show up at the store on her first day, but I just couldn't stay away. As I turned and started the familiar walk toward Flowers on Fairfield, I told myself it was to fill Mom in about Ashley and Olivia being related. But deep down I knew the truth: I was checking up on her.

It was my favorite time of day. The late afternoon sun bathed everything — houses, storefronts, trees, even mailboxes — in its reddish-golden light, making Fairfield Street somehow sharper and more beautiful. When I approached the shop window, at first I couldn't see inside from the glare. Then I got closer and squinted. My heart sank. The window was crammed with bud vases, and each one held a different colored gerbera daisy. It was very colorful.

And very disorganized.

The bell rang as I pushed the door open. The store was empty. No hello. No "Welcome to Flowers on Fairfield." Where was Mom? I felt a pang of worry.

She came running out from the back, Gran's flowered apron tied around her waist. "I'm so sorry . . ." she started. Then she laughed. "Oh, it's you!" She pointed to the front window. "What do you think of the new display?" She nearly bounced on her toes with anticipation.

I sighed, no longer worried, but a little bit frustrated. "Mom, you should really greet the customers the minute they walk in the door!" I said. "And did you use every bud vase in the store for the display?"

Mom's face fell. *Shut up, Del*, I thought. *It's her first day. Give her a chance.* But I kept going.

"What if we need one for an order?" I asked.

Mom sank back onto her heels, looking disappointed.

"You have to think about these things, Mom!"

Then I caught sight of the worktable, and I gasped. I struggled to keep quiet, but the words just flew out. "Mom!" I cried. "This is such a mess! Gramps would have a fit if he saw this!"

Mom sighed. "I was busy all day doing the weekly arrangements for Oscar's, and didn't get to clean up yet," she said.

I wondered how those had turned out. Oscar's was the fanciest restaurant in town, and had been a client of Gran and Gramps's for years.

"And I'm still getting used to everything," Mom went on. "Don't worry, it will all fall into place." She thought for a moment and then her face brightened. "I got three new walk-in customers just from my window display! They told me so."

"Okay..." I said, trying to be supportive. But I couldn't

help grabbing a garbage can and tossing stems and leaves into it.

Mom took it from me gently. "Del!" she said. "Relax. Things will be easier and neater in here once Daddy's done with finals."

Yeah, I thought to myself rather meanly, *things will be much better with both Mr.* and *Mrs. Disorganized in charge.* But I managed to keep my mouth shut.

"Go home and do your homework," Mom added. "I'll close up and meet you there."

I looked at her, about to argue.

"Stop worrying, Delphinium," she said firmly. "I can handle this."

I left the store without even getting to tell Mom about Ashley Edwards.

I walked home, my shoulders drooping. I didn't like the way things were going. Not one bit. Then as I reached my house, I felt my spirits lift. Gran and Gramps would be back in three months. As long as the store didn't fall apart before then, everything was going to be okay.

Right?

The next morning, I went down to the kitchen, my stomach growling. Mom makes us a healthy breakfast every morning. She likes to be sure we start the day with a balanced meal. So I blinked in surprise to see Dad manning the stove, a frilly apron around his waist and a whisk in his hand.

"Good morning, my dear," he said. "I trust scrambled eggs will be to your liking?"

"Um . . . sure," I stammered. I glanced at Rose and Aster, who were sitting at the kitchen table in stunned silence.

Just then Poppy made an appearance. "Twenty-two!" she announced. Poppy likes to count each step as she goes downstairs. If you somehow get caught behind her, this ends up taking forever. And she always tells us the number, as if somehow it could change from day to day.

Then she saw Dad. And she wasn't as polite as the rest of us.

"Daddy's cooking?" she wailed. "Yuck!"

"Where's Mom?" I asked.

"In the study, on the phone with Olivia," he said. "For

forty-five minutes now. I realized if you girls were going to get a decent breakfast, I had to step in."

"Great," I said with a sigh.

Here's the deal — Dad is a bad cook. Mom may burn dinner now and then, but when she manages to set the timer, her food is very tasty. Dad, on the other hand, has a special talent for turning ordinary meals like scrambled eggs into something completely gross. It's like his secret, evil superpower. If he were a supervillain he would be Inedible Man — able to destroy appetites with a single dish!

I poured Poppy and myself some orange juice.

"So," said Rose, looking around at all of us. "Does anyone want to ask me how the play is going?"

"How is the play going, Rose?" we all asked in unison.

"I'm glad you asked," she said, fluffing her hair and smiling.

Aster snorted. Rose gave her an elbow to the ribs.

"The play is going great!" Rose went on. "This is the best cast yet, I swear. And I tell you, I was born to play this role. Now" — she paused for dramatic effect — "Aster helped me with my lines when we did *Annie Get Your Gun* last fall, so I was thinking that this time . . ." She smiled in my direction like she was about to give me a large and expensive gift. ". . . Del, would you like to do the honors?"

"Oh!" I said in surprise. "Really?" I thought of a million excuses not to do it. Rose can be demanding, and running through the same dialogue over and over is crazy boring. But my sister was looking at me so hopefully that I had to say, "I would love to."

"I'm glad that's settled," said Rose, spreading a paper napkin daintily on her lap. "Now we have to figure out how not to eat breakfast," she said in a low voice.

"Voilà!" said Dad, presenting us with a towering platter of gray eggs. "I don't know why I don't do this more often," he said. "This cooking thing is pretty fun!"

Aster bravely ate a forkful, but the look on her face was enough for me. She slipped the rest into her napkin. Rose put hers back on the platter while Dad's back was turned, then hurried out of the kitchen. Poppy tried to feed hers to Buster, but even he was not interested.

Just then Mom swept in, still on her cell phone. She balanced it on her shoulder as she poured coffee into a thick, purple mug I had made for her in pottery class. "That's great, Olivia. Okay, don't worry. Everything will be fine. Just think about what I said. Okay, good-bye." Mom snapped the phone shut and sat down at the table.

"Well, she's certainly a handful," she said, slathering raspberry jam on a cold piece of toast. "She's freaking out about the centerpieces and we haven't even talked themes or colors yet. I suggested she might want to get a wedding planner to help her." She poured some milk into her coffee and stirred it. "I hope she takes my advice," she added with a sigh.

"I know she's a pain," I told Mom as I got up from the table, my napkin concealing the uneaten eggs on my plate. "But just remember, she's our customer and the customer is always right, no matter what." I hurriedly dumped the eggs in the trash, rinsed my plate, and placed it in the dishwasher.

Mom stood up and kissed me on both cheeks. "You've learned very well from your grandparents, Del," she said. "It's just that Olivia is such a . . ."

"Bridezilla," we both said together.

"Grrrr!" said Poppy delightedly, baring her teeth and curling her hands into claws.

I didn't want to admit it to myself, but when I got to school, I was totally looking for Señor Guapo, I mean, Mr.

Do-Si-Do. (Or maybe I should call him Mr. Do-Si-Don't, considering my squashed toes.) I told myself I just felt bad for him because he didn't know anyone.

It wasn't until lunchtime that I saw him on the other line in the cafeteria. He had a hamburger, French fries, and three, count 'em, three chocolate milks on his tray. Not that it was any of my business, but you have to admit, that is a lot of chocolate milk, growing boy or not. I briefly considered calling his name and inviting him to sit with me and my friends, but before I got up the nerve, he had disappeared into the crowded lunchroom.

I joined Becky at our usual table, sitting with our friends Jessica Wu, Amy Arthur, and Heather. As soon as I sat down, Becky leaned forward eagerly and started to talk. But her mouth was full and I couldn't understand a word she was saying.

"Chew!" I said, laughing.

She swallowed her mac and cheese and started over. "I forgot to tell you something last night on the phone!" she said.

"Go on," I said, unwrapping my chicken salad sandwich.

Becky shivered with excitement. As the daughter of the "About Town" columnist (Becky's mom *hates* to be called a gossip columnist, but technically, that's what she is), Becky loves to share a good story.

"My mom told me that there's going to be a cover story on Olivia and her fiancé in the Stylish Times section!" she said breathlessly.

"Wait, who's Olivia?" Jessica wanted to know, running her hand through her jet-black pixie cut. She dresses supergirly, mostly in short skirts and leggings, so no one ever mistakes her for a boy.

Becky looked like she was about to burst as I hit the pause button and filled our three friends in.

The Stylish Times is the section in the local newspaper that features all the wedding announcements, fundraisers, fancy parties, concerts, and openings that happen in town. It's a big deal to certain people to get featured in it. *Olivia must be totally excited,* I thought.

Once everyone was up-to-date, Becky continued. "And get this — remember last year when that revival of *The Sound of Music* came to town with that famous singing lady and everyone in town was fighting over tickets?"

"That's right," I said. Rose had begged my parents to get tickets, but they hadn't been able to.

"Oh, I remember!" said Amy, looking studious in her new rectangular glasses. The glasses looked good with her pale skin and reddish hair, but I still hadn't gotten used to her wearing them. "My mother was so mad she didn't get to go."

"A lot of people were," Becky said. "My mom got an entire column out of that one!"

"So what does *The Sound of Music* have to do with Olivia?" I wondered. I pulled open my barbecue potato chip bag, fished out a chip, and crunched it. Yum.

"Well, Olivia went to the concert with her boyfriend at the time. And she *just so happened* to be seated next to a very handsome man who was there on a date himself. But for Olivia and the handsome guy, it was love at first sight. By the final curtain call they had exchanged e-mail addresses. And now they're getting married."

"Ooh!" squealed Amy. "That is sooooo romantic!"

I licked orange barbecue powder off my fingers. "Not for their dates, it wasn't!" I said.

Becky let out a yelp. "You're right, Del!"

"Oh man!" said Heather.

I guess it wasn't particularly *funny* for their dates, either. But we all got a good laugh out of it. We had to explain it to Jessica, who can be a bit of a space cadet, but when she got it she laughed, too.

"What's so funny?" said a voice.

I looked up to see Ashley standing by our table, wearing her usual snotty expression.

"None of your business," I replied.

Ashley shook her head at the bag of chips in front of me. "I can't believe you eat that stuff, Delphinium," she said. "Yuck!"

I ignored her and shook a couple more chips into my mouth. "Mmm-mmmm good," I said, smacking my lips. I smiled sweetly at her. "Can we help you, Ashley?"

Ashley tossed her hair proudly. "I just wanted to let you know something totally fab," she began. I gritted my teeth. "The guest list has been finalized for the wedding." She smiled. "Five hundred people are invited."

What? My heart skipped a beat. *That's a lot of centerpieces for one small store to make!* But I tried not to let my panic show on my face.

"And," she continued, "you do remember that the groom's father is the mayor, don't you? As you can imagine, there are several very important people invited."

"Oh yeah, like who?" I asked. "The town dog-catcher?"

Ashley rolled her eyes. "Hel-lo, Delphinium. Like the fire chief and the entire city council?"

"How exciting for you," I said.

"And we've been dress shopping for superexpensive bridesmaids dresses," she added. She eyed my faded jeans, vintage Snoopy T-shirt, orange cardigan, and my favorite Vans with the multicolored robots on them. "One dress will probably cost more than your whole wardrobe." She paused, then added, "I really hope you guys can handle this wedding!"

Now what was my comeback? Oh yeah! "Calm down, Tinky Winky," I said. But Ashley was already headed back to her table, her off-white suede boots click-clacking on the lunchroom floor.

"That was funny, Del," said Becky supportively. The rest of my friends nodded. But it was too little too late.

Chapter Five

It was the first Saturday — my full day at the shop — since Gran and Gramps had left. Mom and I headed out bright and early, grabbing breakfast bars from the kitchen on our way. Dad was already tying on his frilly apron, and I was glad to have an excuse to skip another of his culinary creations.

"I think today should go well," Mom said as we set off down the front steps.

"I'm sure it will," I said absentmindedly. Then I turned to her. "Wait, what do you mean? Is something special happening today?"

"Olivia finally hired a wedding planner!" she said happily. "And the planner is going bridesmaid dress shopping with Olivia and her friends this morning. So when Olivia comes in to the store this afternoon she should know her colors and we can get started choosing flowers!"

"Wait, Olivia is coming in today?" I asked. "Alone?" I added hopefully.

"No, I think she'll have her bridal party with her," Mom said.

"Mom!" I cried. "Why didn't you tell me?"

"I'm sure I did . . ." Mom said. She shrugged. "Or maybe I forgot to. Does it really make a difference, anyway?"

The difference was that if I knew we were having a special meeting — possibly with *Ashley* there — I would not be dressed up like a reject from that old show Gramps liked to watch called *Hee Haw*. I looked down at my patched jeans and ratty sneakers and briefly considered running home and changing my outfit. I had been planning on cleaning out the flower refrigerator that day and had dressed accordingly. I hadn't even washed my hair.

"You're never going to believe this," I told Mom with a sigh, "but it turns out that Ashley Edwards is Olivia's cousin. So there's a chance she might be there today."

Mom grimaced as we crossed the street. She knows how much I dislike Ashley. "I can open up by myself," she said. "Do you want to run home and change?"

I mentally started going through my wardrobe and assembling a cool yet casual outfit, then stopped myself. "No way," I concluded. "If I change my clothes, then it's like I care what she thinks." I quickly pulled out the two pigtails I was wearing and combed my fingers through my hair. "This look says I don't care at all."

Mom seemed like she was trying not to laugh.

"I'm overthinking this, aren't I?" I asked.

"Well, maybe just a bit," Mom admitted. Then she grinned. "I can't believe Pinky Dinky is Olivia's cousin!"

I shook my head and laughed. "Oh, Mom," I said.

After we settled in, Mom sat down behind the counter and began flipping through her sketchbook. I opened the refrigerator door and started cleaning up stray petals and leaves from the floor. It was chilly work. The whole time I kept thinking, *Please, Olivia, leave your junior bridesmaid at home today!*

At precisely 2:14 (the appointment was at 1:30, but who was keeping track? Besides me, that is.) Olivia entered the store, her engagement ring flashing like a paparazzi's flashbulb. A seemingly endless line of people followed her inside. There were fourteen, yes, I said *fourteen* of her closest friends, all of them as pretty and polished as Olivia herself. There was her mom and grandmother. And, I was sorry to see, one obnoxious twelve-year-old cousin, dressed to the nines. She was wearing a fake fur vest (at least I assumed it was fake, but with Ashley you never know) over a ribbed turtleneck. Black jeans and ankle boots completed the outfit.

She said nothing, but gave me the up and down and curled her lip.

Maybe I *should* have gone home and changed.

The store was now packed with chattering women. The mingled scent of hair spray and perfume canceled out the usual sweet flowery smell.

Mom looked around wildly. "Um, Olivia, where's your wedding planner?" she asked. Then she grew serious. "You did get one, didn't you?"

Olivia laughed a tinkly little laugh. "Oh yes!" she said. "I think she had to stop off at the pharmacy for something. She said she'd meet us here."

The bell over the door jingled and an older woman walked in. She wore a bright red coat, towering black pumps, and bright red lipstick. Her jet-black hair was pulled back into a severe bun.

"Hello, I'm Corinne Jacobsen, the wedding planner," she said. "Can I get a glass of water, please?" she asked, holding up a bottle of aspirin.

Mom and I looked at each other, our eyes wide. If the wedding planner had a headache, then the bridesmaid dress selection had not gone well at all.

And that didn't bode well for us.

I pulled a couple of folding chairs from the back room, but there weren't nearly enough places for people to sit, so we had bridesmaids all over the place, perched on one another's laps and sitting cross-legged on the floor. I stood in the corner, carefully positioning myself so I could avoid having to look at Ashley, who sat at her cousin's feet.

Mom got Corinne a cup of water, then stood in front of the group, her hands clasped, waiting for everyone to settle down. Finally, one enterprising bridesmaid stuck two fingers into her mouth and let out a whistle. Everyone quieted immediately. I stared at the girl admiringly. I could never figure out how to do that. And not for lack of trying, either. It would come in handy with my family.

"Welcome to Flowers on Fairfield!" Mom said, her voice a bit shaky. I clasped my hands together anxiously. As I learned in English class when we did public speaking, there is nothing worse than listening to someone who is nervous speak. It puts you on edge, too.

Calm down, I thought, trying to send Mom a message. *You can do this.*

"We are so excited to be a part of your special day, Olivia," she continued.

Olivia nodded and beamed.

"So I wanted to hear how dress shopping went this morning," Mom went on in her fake cheerful voice. "Have you settled on a color?"

Everyone started to jabber at once. Mom kept smiling, but her neck was starting to turn bright red. I had the sudden terrified feeling that she was going to throw up all over the wedding planner, who had managed to snag one of the chairs and was sitting right in front of her.

Olivia rolled her eyes. "No one can agree on anything!" she whined.

"Well, that pink dress with the tulle skirt was totally perfect!" said a dark-haired bridesmaid with hoop earrings.

"Yeah," agreed the bridesmaid who had whistled.

"That's because you two look good in pink," scoffed a redhead. "And I don't!"

"That's just a myth," said the dark-haired girl.

The redhead gave her the evil eye. "Have you ever seen me in pink?" she asked. "I look like a baked ham."

Olivia shuddered.

"Now that emerald green dress . . ." started the redhead.

"Yuck!" called out a petite blonde. "I look like a corpse in green!"

The wedding planner stood up. "Ladies!" she cried, raising a hand to her temple. "Let's remember whose special day this is."

Olivia smiled at her. "That's right," she said. "If you don't all stop arguing, I'm going to pick that yellow taffeta dress you *all* hated."

There was a collective gasp and everyone shut up.

The silence was broken by Olivia's grandmother, a sweet-looking lady in a pale blue suit.

"That redheaded gal *did* look like a canned ham!" she said in a superloud whisper.

"Mom! Turn up your hearing aid!" cried Olivia's mother.

Everyone burst into laughter, including the redhead. "I told you!" she said.

"Ladies!" called Corinne again. "Need I remind you that the dresses need to be ordered this weekend? We have to come to some decision or you're all going to be walking down the aisle naked on May nineteenth!" She looked at Mom. "And we can't order the flowers until we decide on a color!"

What a mess! I craned my neck to steal a glance at Ashley, who was sitting on the floor looking smug. That made me mad. She was actually *enjoying* the fact that things were spiraling out of control!

I stared at Mom, silently begging her to speak up. *This wouldn't be happening if Gran and Gramps were here,* I thought. *We are going to lose this wedding if she doesn't do something fast.* But Mom looked defeated. Olivia and her friends weren't giving her anything to work with. There were too many opinionated people in one room. Olivia just needed to make up her own mind. Suddenly I had an idea.

I cleared my throat. "Olivia," I said. She turned around and looked at me quizzically. So did everyone else, Mom included. I gulped, but kept talking. "Suppose you were walking down Fairfield Street and decided to stop in our store and buy yourself a bouquet of flowers. What colors would you choose?"

Olivia thought for a moment. "I like bright colors," she decided. "Purples, pinks, and reds."

Catching on, Mom gave me a grateful smile. She walked over to the flower refrigerator and began pulling out red sweet peas, purple anemones, and some bright pink roses. She cut the stems and began arranging them this way and that. "This is one of my favorite color combinations," she said. "Bold, beautiful, very joyful." She began wrapping bright pink ribbon around the stems. Then she got a kind of *aha!* light in her eyes and turned around so no one could see what she was doing. I fidgeted nervously. Mom was either going to come up with something that would knock Olivia's socks off. Or she was about to lose the sale forever.

When Mom turned around I saw that she had tucked

several strawberries that were left over from our lunch into the center of the bouquet.

"Ta-da!" she said.

"Strawberries?" said Mrs. Post. "How interesting!" And by "interesting" I am pretty sure she meant "bizarre."

"Yes," said Mom. "I think that fruit adds a fresh and fun element. The bouquet is playful, yet elegant."

Sure, it looked pretty. Pretty strange, too. What would Olivia say?

Olivia stared at the flowers, her brow wrinkled. Mom handed the bouquet to a cute brown-haired girl wearing a navy blue sweater dress, who obligingly held the flowers bridesmaid-style, waist high. The flowers really stood out against the dark background.

"Have you thought about neutrals?" Mom asked. "See how the flowers pop against the rich navy blue of her dress?"

A smile spread across Olivia's face. "Yes!" she said excitedly. She looked around at all her bridesmaids. "And navy blue looks good on everyone!"

"I do look good in navy," agreed the redheaded bridesmaid. "Plus, I went to ten weddings last year and *no one* did fruit." She nodded solemnly. "It's very unique."

This sealed the deal for Olivia. "It's . . . perfect!" she cried.

Relief shot through me, and everyone sighed with happiness. Everyone except Ashley, that is, who was staring at me with open hostility. I smiled at her sweetly, which I knew burned her up inside. *Too bad for you, Ashley*, I thought. *Flowers on Fairfield is back in business!*

"Ladies?" said Corinne the wedding planner. "Remember that silk chiffon empire-waist dress? Totally flattering and it definitely comes in navy. That bouquet would look amazing against it."

Olivia looked around at the bridesmaids. They were all jostling one another to take a turn holding the beautiful bouquet. "That's it!" she said. "Let's go back to the store right now so they can take everyone's measurements!"

As everyone began to get on their coats and grab their purses, talking excitedly, Mom and I grinned at each other.

But my happiness was short-lived. Because the shop bell jangled. And to my annoyance, in walked Rose, Aster, and Poppy. What were *they* doing here?

Poppy immediately ran up to my mom, wrapping

herself around her leg and hanging on for dear life. The bridesmaids all oohed and ahhed. "How cute!" they exclaimed.

"What are you doing with all these ladies?" Poppy wanted to know while Rose and Aster whispered to each other about who knows what.

When Mom explained that Olivia was getting married, Poppy disentangled herself and walked over to Olivia. "A wedding!" she cried. "Then you need a flower girl." She cocked her head at Olivia. "Pick me!"

I groaned.

"So sweet!" said a bridesmaid.

Olivia laughed and told Poppy she had already promised the job to her fiancé's niece, but that Poppy could be her alternate.

"That's like being an understudy!" exclaimed Rose. "If the flower girl can't perform on the day of the wedding, then the part belongs to you!"

This seemed to satisfy my little sister and she retreated behind the counter. I stole a glance at Mom, but she didn't look embarrassed by Poppy at all. I seemed to be the only one who was totally mortified.

But just as Olivia was about to leave, Poppy came rushing back over.

"Bride lady!" my sister squealed. "I want to ask you a question!"

Olivia leaned down so she was at Poppy's level. "Yes?" she asked.

"Where's your tail?" Poppy asked in all seriousness.

Olivia wrinkled her nose in confusion. "My tail?" she said.

"Yeah, your tail," said Poppy. "I thought you would have a tail."

As Olivia smiled and turned away, my stomach sank. Surely Poppy wasn't about to say what I thought she was about to . . .

"You sure don't *look* like Godzilla!"

Mom and I glanced at each other in dread. I'm sure my eyes were bugging out as much as Mom's were. Luckily, Olivia had left just in time and hadn't heard. But someone else had.

"Godzilla, huh?" said Ashley. She gave me a knowing smirk and walked out the door.

Chapter Six

School was over for the day and we were all crowded in the hall, doing the usual locker gymnastics. Everyone was maneuvering around one another, pulling out books and grabbing our coats and backpacks.

"Hello, Delphinium," said Ashley from behind me.

I didn't even look away from my locker. I knew that she'd be standing there, flanked by her handmaidens, and dressed in some fashionable outfit, with an impatient sneer on her face.

"Can I help you, Ashley?" I sighed, looking back at her. Right on all counts. She was wearing matchstick jeans and a soft-looking pink sweater that almost came to her knees. *And* had extralong sleeves with thumbholes. My fingers seemed to have a mind of their own and were practically reaching out to touch it to see if it was cashmere. I folded my hands under my armpits so I wouldn't be tempted.

She leaned in, scowling. "So you think my cousin is a Bridezilla, huh?"

I quickly turned away so she couldn't see my guilty expression. "I have no idea what you're talking about," I said, busying myself in my locker. My stomach was tight with worry.

Ashley tapped me on the shoulder. When I turned around again she had a big smile on her face. "Oh, I think you do," she said. Then she sauntered off with her hand-maidens, and they stopped to whisper in front of a nearby bank of lockers. Rachel leaned against one of the lockers. It belonged to Maria Gonzalez, who at the moment needed to get her trumpet out for band practice. But of course Ashley and her friends didn't notice. I rolled my eyes and turned back to my locker.

Suddenly I heard an annoyingly familiar boy's voice behind me.

"What kind of name is that, anyway?" the boy snorted. "It's just . . . weird."

I nearly mis-shelved my Spanish textbook. Ashley was

bad enough to deal with, but now here was Bob, the bully from gym class.

Bob was the torturer of anyone who could somehow be considered different. This included the bespectacled, the too short or too tall, the kids with braces, the kids who didn't wear "normal" clothes, and as I was well aware, the oddly named. I automatically assumed he was talking to me.

I spoke into my locker as my hands clenched and unclenched. "I thought I told you I was named after . . ." I started to say.

"Well, Bob," said another voice. "I'm named after Alexander Hamilton, one of the Founding Fathers of the United States of America. Heard of him?"

I spun around. It was Hamilton!

Hamilton wasn't getting annoyed and flustered like I did when Bob bothered me. He wasn't throwing his milk carton at him and getting detention like the unfortunately named Dilbert Pickles. No. Hamilton was just standing there, hands in his pockets, casually talking to Bob like he wasn't the dumbest bully in middle school history.

"Um, yeah, I've heard of him," Bob said uncertainly. (With *his* history grades, I seriously doubted that one.)

"But at least I'm not named after him," he added. He looked around for support. Surely, we all agreed Hamilton must be humiliated for allowing his parents to name him something so silly!

Matt, one of Bob's buddies, spoke up. "Is your nickname, um, Ham Sandwich?" he asked Hamilton.

I winced. Talk about dumb and dumber!

"Um . . . no," replied Hamilton. He looked like he was trying hard not to smile.

Bob thought that was hilarious. "Yeah, Ham Sandwich!" he said. "That's your new nickname!"

Hamilton just shrugged, which made Bob even madder. "What, are we boring you, Ham Sandwich?" he asked, getting red in the face.

Suddenly, I found myself walking right up to Bob and Matt. "Excuse me," I said. "Are you guys *always* this unfunny, or is today a special occasion?"

"Shut up, Delfingerprints," Bob muttered.

"And who are you to make fun of people's names?" I went on, pointing my finger in Bob's face. He backed away from me. "I mean, how unoriginal. If you say your name backward, it's still . . . Bob."

Bob scowled. He couldn't argue with that one.

"Good one, Del!" shouted Mike Hurley from where he stood at his locker across the hallway.

"Ham Sandwich!" Mike's best friend, Carmine Rizzo, added with a snort. "That was totally lame!"

"Yeah, completely lame!" Penelope Peterson chimed in. Carmine, who had a huge crush on her, looked pleased.

Bob and Matt looked at me, furious that the tables had been turned. "Well, your names *are* dumb!" Bob finally said, backing down the hall.

"Yeah, walk away!" Mike called after them. "Come back when you can come up with a real insult!"

Hamilton picked up his backpack and walked over to me. "Wow, Del," he said, his eyebrows raised. "That was quick!"

I shook my head. "I can never come up with anything when *I'm* the one being picked on!" I admitted.

"What a jerk," he said. "I don't get guys like that. They feel better by making other people feel bad about themselves."

I nodded, thinking about Ashley. She could never resist an opportunity to make me look silly in front of other people. "Welcome to Sarah Josepha Hale Middle School," I said.

"Well, you showed Bob," Hamilton said. "I bet it will be a day or two before he makes fun of you again, Delphinium Bloom!"

I grinned at Hamilton. Then I had to look away. I felt suddenly weirdly self-conscious. *What is wrong with you, Del?* I thought. I focused on his feet, which today were encased in beat-up work boots.

"There's one of him in every school," said Hamilton. "And if you're lucky, there's only one." He looked at me. "It's not so easy having a weird name, is it?"

I shrugged. "Nah." I thought for a moment. "But it beats a lisp," I said.

Hamilton laughed and explained that his dad had picked his name. "He's a history buff and he loves Alexander Hamilton. He's his favorite Founding Father," he added, his eyes lighting up.

I nodded. I didn't know anyone who had a favorite Founding Father. In fact, I'd be surprised if I knew anyone, my college professor dad excluded, who could name them all.

Hamilton was not done extolling the virtues of his namesake. "He led soldiers into battle during the Revolutionary War, he founded the Bank of New York, he was the first secretary of the treasury, and he wrote most of the Federalist Papers," he explained. I made a mental note to Google "Federalist Papers" when I got home. They sounded important. He smiled. "And he also founded the New York Manumission Society to help end slavery," he said. "He was a man ahead of his time."

I searched my brain for any random bits of Alexander Hamilton information I may have stored there. Yes! "Wasn't he killed in a duel?" I asked.

Hamilton's face clouded over. Yikes. Maybe that wasn't the best factoid to start with. "Yeah. Aaron Burr shot him. What a loser."

"Well, Alexander Hamilton sounds really great," I said. I decided to change the subject before I said anything else upsetting. "My weird name is not quite as interesting as yours. I'm just named after a —"

"Flower, I know," said Hamilton. I stared at him, startled, and he smiled at me. "I think Delphinium is a really cool name."

I blushed from the roots of my hair to the tips of my toes. "Um . . . thanks," was all I could come out with. I had never met another kid, let alone a boy, who had ever heard of delphinium before. *How random!* I thought.

Hamilton sighed. "I guess . . . You know, I don't get to see my dad as much as I'd like to since Mom got remarried and we moved here," he said. "So I think that makes me more mad when people make fun of the name he picked, you know?"

"Well, you don't show it," I said. "You seemed so cool about it."

He laughed. "Oh, I was just trying to look cool," he said. "I was pretty mad inside."

My mind started racing. *Who was he trying to look cool in front of?* I wondered. I tried to remember who had been standing in the now nearly empty hallway . . . Penelope Peterson? Maria Gonzalez?

Hamilton threw his backpack over his shoulder and gave me a salute. "Bye, Delphinium. See you tomorrow."

I watched him lope down the hallway, and smiled as he jumped up to hit the EXIT sign above the door at the end of the hall. I smiled all the way home, too.

I was in such a good mood I didn't even complain when I had to set the table for the second night in a row because Rose still wasn't home from rehearsal. And I didn't say anything when Dad announced we were having leftovers again. And it was his tuna casserole, which is bad enough the first night. Hot canned tuna — which culinary genius invented that one?

But as I was loading the dishwasher, I had a sudden, awful thought. I remembered someone else who had been in the hallway that afternoon. Could it be that the person Hamilton was trying to look cool in front of was . . . *Ashley Edwards?*

I wanted to think the boy had better taste than that. But it was a definite — and unpleasant — possibility.

Chapter Seven

The next morning, over hot chocolates in the cafeteria, I filled Becky and Heather in on what happened in the hallway with Ashley — and Hamilton.

"I can't believe you didn't call and tell us last night!" Heather cried, slamming down her copy of *Us Weekly*.

I blushed. I hadn't called Becky or Heather because after dinner I'd done my homework and then stayed up late reading about Alexander Hamilton on Wikipedia.

"I'm just impressed you stood up to Bob," Becky said, her brown eyes widening. "You usually never come up with comebacks until days later!"

"I know," I said. "Isn't that weird?"

Becky beamed. "I'm proud of you, Del!"

But Heather just studied me, a funny look on her face.

"What?" I said.

"I recognize the signs," she said, nodding solemnly. "You've got it bad."

"Got what?" I asked warily.

"A big old crush," she said, smiling at me.

I shook my head at her. "We're just friends, Heather!" I exclaimed.

Heather just kept smiling at me. I sighed. Heather had a new crush every few weeks, so she thought she was an expert. Becky, on the other hand, looked a little disappointed in me. But she had nothing to worry about. I didn't *like* like Hamilton. He was a boy friend. Not a boyfriend. End. Of. Story.

After school I decided to call the store to see if Mom needed any help. Dad answered the phone instead.

"Flowers on Fairfield," he said. "Serving Your Floral Needs Since, um . . ."

"1912," I finished. "It's me, Dad," I said. "How's everything going?"

"Pretty good," he said. "I've been working on the books and I'm happy to say that your grandparents left things in great order." Then he lowered his voice. "Del, did you clean up your mom's work space again?" he asked. "She's a little annoyed."

I winced. I *had* stopped by the store as Mom was closing up the night before and secretly organized her space. It was such a mess — piles of discarded ribbon, soaking-wet floral foam, shears, hot-glue gun all in a jumble. But it seemed as if Mom wasn't very grateful. Not one bit.

"Yes," I said. "I guess she doesn't want to thank me?"

"On the contrary," said Dad. "She's going crazy looking for her shears. And her floral tape."

I explained where she could find them and refrained from adding *Where they belong*. No need to rile anyone up any further! I also decided to skip going to the store that afternoon. I might be tempted to do some more organizing and I knew how well *that* would go over!

In the middle of breakfast the next morning, Mom's cell phone rang. It was the theme from that old movie *Jaws* — you know, da-Dum, da-Dum, da-Dum, da-DUM! Just before the shark attacks.

Mom reached over to the kitchen counter and picked the phone up, looking confused. Her eyebrows rose as she recognized the name on the display.

"Hello, Olivia," she answered. "Of course this isn't a bad time . . ." We all watched as she made a "sorry" face at us and wandered out of the kitchen.

I stared at my sisters. Which one was the ringtone culprit? Rose looked innocent, but she was an actress, I reminded myself. I turned to Aster. She tried to look really busy cutting up her rock-hard waffle, but I could see the mischievous look in her eye.

I glowered at the two of them, since the twins rarely worked alone. "*Jaws?*" I said, shaking my head. "Very unprofessional."

Rose shook her head back at me. "You are no fun," she said.

"Totally," added Aster.

That stung. Who wants to be thought of as un-fun?

I looked at Dad. "May I be excused?" I asked.

He put his hand over his heart. "'All happiness depends on a leisurely breakfast'!" he quoted dramatically. "John Gunther."

I apologized and left the kitchen, grabbing Buster's leash from the doorknob. Sometimes I just needed a break from all the Blooms.

That was not the last family meal that Olivia would interrupt. She called a few times a week, sometimes every day. Even though she had her wedding planner, she liked to run things by Mom, too. She said she "trusted her taste."

It turned out that Mom liked the idea of a special ringtone just for Olivia so she was always mentally prepared when the phone rang (or, I suspected, so she could send her calls straight to voice mail). So I helped Mom change it to the more appropriate "Here Comes the Bride." We were all pretty sick of that song after a while. One day, Olivia had flipped out because she hated her headpiece and couldn't find one that she liked. The next day she didn't like the song she and her fiancé had picked for their first dance. And she changed her mind about the shade of the flowers in the centerpieces a million times.

One night I heard Mom on the phone, saying to Olivia: "Well, I don't know if the roses will match the exact shade of pink in tonight's sunset. But we'll try our best."

Olivia really *was* a Bridezilla. Though we never used that word in Poppy's presence again, just to be safe.

One rare phone call–free morning, we sat at the kitchen table finishing up breakfast. We had opted for cold cereal despite Dad's insistence that he would make "tasty French toast."

"So I was thinking tonight felt like a *Muppet Movie* kind of night," said Dad, looking up from the newspaper.

"Huh?" I said.

"For Movie Night," Dad said. "And how about some rocky road?"

I stared at him. Was he for real?

"Movie Night," he repeated. "You know, we do it every Friday?"

Mom spoke up. "Well, maybe Dad's right," she said slowly. "There's no reason not to continue with Movie Night . . ."

I stood up, feeling a lump in my throat. "No way," I said. "Movie Night is what we do with Gran and Gramps. End of story."

Everyone stared at me.

After a moment, Dad shrugged. "Okay, okay," he said. "But it would be a lot of fun . . ."

I sat back down and shook my head. And then we all went back to eating our Rice Krispies in silence. Though I did notice Rose and Aster exchanging glances. I don't understand Twin, so I had no idea what they were saying to each other. Maybe they thought I was being unreasonable. But I didn't care.

At school that afternoon, I sat on a bench in the locker room, tying my sneakers. My gym uniform was freshly laundered (and ironed!) and smelled like fabric softener. I was even wearing matching yellow socks.

Not that I was trying to look good for anyone.

I marched into the gymnasium and sat down in my spot. I turned around and waved to Hamilton, who gave me his trademark lazy grin back.

Tweet! Mr. Rolando blasted his whistle. "I have an announcement to make," he said when he had everyone's attention. "It seems that one of our students has broken his leg skateboarding and will be excused from gym class until his cast is off."

I scanned the room to see who was missing, and real-ized it was Bob the bully.

"So that means that Ashley Edwards needs a new part-ner," Mr. Rolando added.

Ashley tried to look concerned about Bob's well-being, but couldn't hold back the big smile that spread across her face. My heart sank. I knew what was coming. There was only one student in class who didn't have a permanent partner.

"Hamilton, would you please partner up with Ashley?" said Mr. Rolando. "Places, everyone. We're going to start with 'Duck for the Oyster.'"

We all rose to our feet, but I just wanted to disappear.

"Howdy partner," said Ashley flirtatiously as Hamilton ambled up to her. She slipped her hands in his.

I tried not to cringe as Rodney placed his clammy hands in mine. This was going to be a long afternoon.

After school I stopped by the store. We had just gotten a delivery of roses and Mom was removing the thorns and lower leaves. I cleared my throat. "You know, Mom, when Gramps de-thorned roses he always —"

"I'm fine," Mom snapped.

"Is something wrong?" I asked.

Mom closed her eyes. "I'm sorry, Del. I'm just on edge. Olivia was supposed to come in hours ago to drop off her deposit." She looked at her watch, and grabbed a rose stem. "Ow!" she cried. She put her thumb in her mouth. "It just doesn't make sense," Mom went on, reaching for the first-aid kit to retrieve a Band-Aid. "She called me four times yesterday. The wedding is in a couple of weeks. So why isn't she here today? I wonder if there's a problem."

"Oh, there's a problem all right," said a familiar voice. We both looked up.

Aunt Lily, perfectly pulled together as always, stood in front of us. She looked even more serious than usual.

I stared at her. "Where did . . ."

"I came in the back entrance," explained Aunt Lily, cutting me off. "The problem is that there's a new florist in town. It's called Fleur."

"Floor?" I scoffed. "That's a dumb name."

Aunt Lily gave me a withering glance. "Fleur," she repeated icily. "As in the French word for 'flower.'"

"Oh," I said sheepishly. "I take Spanish."

Aunt Lily shook her head, annoyed. "It's in the mall. Where the Nut Hut used to be. And apparently Olivia Post is considering them as her florist for the wedding!"

"*What?*" I cried.

Mom looked stricken. "But how . . ." she started to ask.

"Ethel Murray had lunch with Olivia's grandmother today and she mentioned it. Ethel called me immediately, of course." Aunt Lily looked at me sharply. "What's so funny, Del?"

I couldn't help myself. *Old Lady Mafia strikes again!* I thought to myself, but I quickly wiped the smile off my face. "Nothing is funny, Aunt Lily," I said. "Nothing at all."

Mom groaned. "This is terrible!" she cried, burying her face in her hands.

"This is disastrous," clarified Aunt Lily. "What are you going to do?"

"What *can* I do?" said Mom.

"Call her right now," said Aunt Lily.

Mom picked up the phone and dialed Olivia's number. She snapped the phone shut after a minute. "Straight to voice mail," she said. My stomach tightened. It was official. Olivia was avoiding us.

"Call her again," demanded Aunt Lily. "Leave a message."

Mom sighed and picked up her phone.

An idea came to me then. The mall was close by. And what could be so special about this Fleur place, anyway? There was only one way to find out.

I hated to leave Mom with mean Aunt Lily (and a shipment of roses) but I knew what I had to do. "I'll be right back," I said. Mom just nodded.

I ran home as fast as I could. My bike was in the shed. It hadn't been ridden all winter, but luckily I didn't have a flat. I hopped on my bike and rode straight to Becky's house. She answered the door in her jeans and slippers.

"Hey, Del," she said. "What's up?"

"There's a new florist in town and they've stolen away our Bridezilla," I said quickly. "I need you to help me spy on them."

"Okay," said Becky, quickly ditching her slippers and pulling on her sneakers. One of the many reasons Becky is my best friend: She is always up for an adventure, no questions asked. "Sounds cool."

Minutes later, we were pedaling over to the mall. Once we got there, we locked up our bikes in the rack and went inside. I could smell freshly baked soft pretzels, my favorite snack of all time. But I managed to walk right by the stand. I was on a mission.

Aunt Lily was right. The Nut Hut, which had been out of business for at least six months, was now a flower shop. A big GRAND OPENING sign hung in the window. An arch of white and silver balloons framed the door. I shook my head. After all these years, Flowers on Fairfield finally had some competition. And the timing could not have been worse.

Becky and I huddled in front of Kiddie Kasuals, whispering to each other. "We've got to come up with a story," I told her.

She was excited. "Right! Our cover!" She thought for a moment. "Let's say we're adopted sisters who are buying a birthday present for our mom," she said.

"Creative," I replied. "But potential for disaster. We don't have a lot of time to get our story straight."

Becky nodded, disappointed.

I thought for a moment. "Let's say your grandma's

birthday is coming up and you are thinking of sending her flowers."

Becky frowned. "That's boring because it's true!" she said.

"But it's easy," I said.

"We're spying, Del," said Becky. "It's not supposed to be easy."

I was about to argue with her (since when was Becky a spying expert?) but it was getting late. So I took a deep breath and headed inside.

My heart sank as I looked around. The place was huge, at least twice as big as my family's store. Sleek and shiny with lots of polished chrome. The floor was made of dark cement slabs that looked unfinished and dirty to me, but were probably the height of interior design. The flower cooler was gigantic, and packed with a dozen different kinds of roses. There were some blooms so exotic I had never even seen them before. There were also aisles and aisles of gifts — designer chocolates, retro-looking hand-made stuffed animals, scented candles, and a whole row of potted orchids so beautiful (and expensive) they took my breath away. It was the exact opposite of Flowers on

Fairfield. Even the name — *Fleur* — was sleek and cool compared to the unwieldy and old-fashioned *Flowers on Fairfield*. Flowers on Fairfield was the rotary phone to Fleur's iPhone. Flowers on Fairfield was the horse and buggy to Fleur's . . .

"Can I help you?" My dark thoughts were interrupted by a tall woman with blonde hair, who stood smiling at us.

"It's my birthday!" Becky burst out. "I mean it's my grandmother's birthday!" She glanced around wildly. "She likes flowers!"

I looked at Becky in alarm. My friend had a lot of talents, but espionage was apparently not one of them.

Once Becky had gotten her story straight, the woman took us over to a brand-new computer sitting on a shiny table. "Now, obviously, we can design a beautiful bouquet for your grandmother," she said. "But any flower shop can do that. What makes Fleur so special is this . . ." She clicked the mouse and a page opened up. "This is where you can design a virtual bouquet," she explained. "You click here" — she demonstrated — "to pick your container — vase, basket, planter, jar, you name it. Then you fill your virtual vase with your flowers and arrange them however you want to. Then you can add ribbons, balloons, stuffed animals, or candy, if you like. Then you hit the CREATE button, and we will design your bouquet to your exact specifications. Part of the service here at Fleur, the florist for the twenty-first century!"

I wondered if that was a dig at the competition, since Flowers on Fairfield, *Serving Your Floral Needs Since 1912*, is pretty much the florist for the early twentieth century.

Despite myself, my fingers itched to design a virtual bouquet. Becky reached for the mouse at the same time, but I won. I had just chosen a tall, fluted vase and was considering my floral options when the store's phone rang.

"I'll be right back," the woman said pleasantly.

I was trying to decide between dendrobium and calypso orchids when I heard the blonde woman say something that made my blood freeze.

"Thank you, Corinne," she said into the phone. "I look forward to seeing you and Olivia tonight at five o'clock. I can personally guarantee that Fleur will create the wedding of her dreams!"

Chapter Eight

Becky looked at me, wide-eyed, and I could only stare back at her in shock. So it *was* true — we'd lost our biggest customer! Mom was going to be so disappointed. I felt terrible.

The blonde woman hung up the phone and walked back over to us. "Is everything okay?" she asked, seeing our wan expressions.

"Um, we have to go home now," said Becky. "Our mom is . . . I mean my mom . . . uh, my grandma . . ." Her voice trailed off. "We have to go home," she repeated lamely.

And I couldn't criticize Becky for her fumbling, because I wasn't even capable of forming words at that point.

The woman seemed confused for a moment. Then she smiled and handed us each a magnet with the Fleur website's URL on it. "You can design your virtual bouquet at home!" she said. "As long as you have a major credit card. And your parents' permission."

I took the magnet and shoved it in my pocket. "Thank you," I said miserably.

I waited until we had exited the mall before I spoke.

"Ashley!" I hissed as we unlocked our bikes.

"Huh?" said Becky.

"I know what happened," I muttered, fuming. "Ashley told Olivia that we call her Bridezilla behind her back," I said. "So Olivia changed florists."

"You really think so?" said Becky.

"Oh, I know so," I said. "I bet Ashley even told her all about Fleur. You know how much time Ashley spends at the mall."

"Maybe," said Becky thoughtfully.

After I dropped Becky off at home, I pedaled back to the store in furious silence. Ashley was without question the most awful person I had ever met in my life. It was bad enough when she was mean to me. But to take away my family's business — that was inexcusable. Just thinking about it made my blood boil.

"This is very bad. Very bad!" said Aunt Lily, pacing back and forth in front of the counter. I had just filled her and Mom in on my store visit. "Twice as big! Twice as many flowers! Visual bouquets!"

"Virtual," I corrected.

Aunt Lily glared at me. "And they've stolen the biggest wedding of the year right from under our noses!" She turned to Mom. "Our store is in big trouble," she said. "We could go out of business. Your parents never should have left."

Mom just looked crestfallen. After Aunt Lily walked out, muttering to herself, I helped Mom put the flowers back in the cooler before we closed for the night.

"True, Olivia was a handful," Mom said with a sigh as she locked the front door. "But I put a lot of work into her wedding. And it was such a big order! Fifty centerpieces!" she said. Her shoulders sagged. "I can't believe it," she added sadly. "What a disappointment."

I balled my hands into fists. I didn't have the heart to tell Mom about the Ashley connection. The afternoon had been hard enough as it was.

I walked my bike between us as we made our way home. "Do you think we should tell Gran and Gramps?" I asked.

Mom, Dad, and I had decided that we wouldn't bother Gran and Gramps with work stuff unless it was a life-or-death emergency. Otherwise, Dad said, they'd come running back to fix things. But this was starting to feel a little like life or death to me. Maybe it was time.

Mom shook her head. "There's nothing they can do," she said. "It will only worry them. They'll find out soon enough."

"But is Aunt Lily right? Can we lose the business?" I couldn't imagine us closing up Flowers on Fairfield . . . for good. There was just no way.

"I don't know, Del," she said. "But it will happen whether or not we bother Gran and Gramps. So let's let them get settled before we tell them the bad news."

"All right," I said. We walked home the rest of the way in silence. The only sound was my squeaky front wheel. I'd have to do something about that when I got home.

To say I was distracted at school the next couple of days was the understatement of the year. I accidentally took Aster's homework folder to school with me. (She was not very happy about that, as she got in trouble.) I forgot my lunch money. My teacher called on me in Spanish class and I answered, "rosa," with the correct accent and everything, which means pink. Which would have been fine if I were answering her previous question, which had been *What color is your shirt?* But as the class (including, I noticed, my dear friend Amy) roared with laughter, Señora Jankowski explained that I had actually answered her next question, which was *What color are your eyes?* You can understand my embarrassment. How often does your *teacher* laugh at you?

Gym class was the worst. I was forced to watch Ashley and Hamilton dancing together, and having a great time. Hamilton's square dancing had not improved one bit. He circled left when he was supposed to go right. His allemandes were all over the place. But that didn't seem to bother Ashley. She giggled all class long. And that just made me more and more annoyed. Especially now that I knew the truth about what she'd done.

Friday afternoon, Ashley came up to me by my locker and put her hands on her hips. "It's offish," she said.

"Huh?" I asked even though I had an idea of what she was talking about. I could feel myself start to get worked up.

She rolled her eyes. "*Official.* Olivia's going with Fleur for her flowers. You know, that really gorgeous new florist in the mall?" She shook her head sadly. "I am so sorry you lost the wedding of the year," she added. "But in the long run, I think it's better for all involved. Imagine the things that probably would have gone wrong. It's probably best to leave the flowers to the professionals."

I spun around, my face hot with anger. This was it. I opened my mouth, ready to yell at Ashley for turning Olivia against us. For ruining everything.

But then I stopped myself. *Rise above it, Del,* I said to myself. *Don't give her the satisfaction.* I took a big breath, and tried to pretend I was Rose, acting in a play. Playing the part of someone who didn't care.

"Easy come, easy go," I said with a shrug.

Ashley looked disappointed. She tossed her hair back. "Well, um, all that's left now is the headpiece," she said. "Olivia and I are going shopping this weekend."

"That's great," I said, forcing a yawn.

Ashley frowned, clearly waiting for me to get upset. But I wouldn't give her the satisfaction. As she turned on her heel and marched off down the hall, I wished I *really* didn't care that we'd lost Olivia to Fleur. But I did care. A lot.

Not even stopping at the store on the way home helped my mood. I walked inside to find Poppy behind the counter.

"Hi, Del!" she cried.

"Hey, Poppy," I replied, walking up to the counter. "I thought she was with her babysitter this afternoon," I said to Mom.

"Del!" said Mom, surprised. She sounded almost guilty. "I wasn't expecting you!" She shrugged. "Poppy misses me. I used to be home all the time with her, remember? I figured we could spend some time together here at the shop. She really loves it."

"I'm practicing," said Poppy, all seriousness. She reached into the basket that hung over her arm, pulled out a handful of rose petals, and tossed them into the air. I bit my lip, deciding it was best not to tell Poppy that her chances of being a flower girl were pretty slim now.

Mom grinned. "Isn't she so cute?" she asked me. "I missed her, too," she confessed.

I didn't want to hurt Poppy's feelings, so I pulled Mom to the back of the store, to talk to her in private. "Are you serious?" I asked her. "I mean, I love Poppy, but it's unprofessional to have her behind the counter! It's no wonder . . ." I stopped.

"It's no wonder what?" Mom asked me sharply, giving me a searching look. I instantly felt awful. Did Mom know I was going to say something about us losing Olivia? I could only look down, my cheeks burning. I didn't mean to be cruel.

Mom sighed, and I glanced back up at her. "Del, I know you take this store seriously. And I appreciate that. But . . ." Her voice trailed off.

"But what?" I said. "Tell me!"

She couldn't look me in the eyes. "You sound just like Aunt Lily."

"Well, maybe Aunt Lily has a point!" I retorted.

I can't believe I just said that, I thought. I didn't want to be like Aunt Lily. Right?

❀   ❀   ❀

That night, over dessert, Mom was all fired up. I wondered if what I'd said to her at the store had had some sort of an effect. "We need to win our bride back!" she declared. She pointed her ice-cream spoon in the air for emphasis. "Flowers on Fairfield will not go down without a fight!"

"Could you offer her a discount?" suggested Dad. "Add a free arrangement for the church or something?"

Mom and I shook our heads at the same time. "Money is not a problem for our bride," she explained. "I don't think that's going to do it."

"It's got to be something special," I said, getting into the spirit. "Something to make her wedding different."

"I know! I know!" shouted Poppy. "I could be a special kind of flower girl who follows her around *all day* throwing flower petals."

"That's just silly," I said.

Poppy made a face and climbed into Mom's lap, almost knocking over her water glass.

"That's a great idea, Poppy," said Mom gently. "But remember, Olivia already has a flower girl." She gave me a stern look over Poppy's head, and I felt bad.

"I could sing at her wedding!" Rose suggested. She stood up and cleared her throat. It doesn't take much to encourage Rose to sing — or dance — in public.

"No thanks, Rose," I said brusquely.

Mom shook her head at me. "That is a lovely idea, Rosie," she said. "But I was thinking we'd do something special with flowers."

Rose smiled at Mom and gave me a dirty look. Aster seconded it.

It was the twins' night to clean up after dinner, so I wandered upstairs to do my homework. But I kept thinking. There had to be some way to win Olivia back.

I just had no idea what it could possibly be.

I went online and started looking at different florist sites for some ideas. A centerpiece that had never been done before. A bouquet unlike any other. But I came up with nothing. I could feel my temperature rising as my oh-so-slow computer took forever to open a website's homepage. This was getting me nowhere. Plus, I had some extra-hard math homework to finish.

There was a knock at the door. I shuffled over and opened it. There stood Rose, two copies of the *Bye Bye*

Birdie script in her hand. "Are you ready to run through my lines?" she asked.

I sighed. "It's not a good time, Rose," I said. "Too much going on. I have to figure out how to win Olivia back. It's really important."

"But you promised you'd help me!" Rose said, her eyes filling with tears.

"Sorry," I said. "Bad timing."

Rose's shoulders drooped as she turned away. "Whatever," she said.

"All right, all right," I said with a sigh. "Name any day next week."

Rose thought for a moment. "Next Tuesday. I don't have play practice that day."

"Okay, I'll be home by four o'clock," I said. I shook my head and closed my door. Little sisters! They thought the world revolved around them.

Much later, I was lying in bed, tossing and turning, going over everything in my head. I thought back to the first few days after Gramps and Gran left, when Mom had just taken over the store and I was so on edge about it — and for good reason! I thought about the espionage trip to Fleur, and what a good friend Becky was. Suddenly, I remembered something else about Becky — something she had told me a couple of weeks ago, during lunch.

I sat bolt upright in bed, then raced downstairs. Buster, who had been sleeping at the top of the staircase, padded after me. He whined in disappointment when I didn't head to the kitchen, but followed me into the family room and promptly fell asleep on the rug. I laughed to myself, then continued on my mission. I opened the door of the entertainment unit and pawed through the jumble of DVDs. I knew it was in there somewhere. We had every Disney movie ever made, it seemed like. Too many Barneys. *A Charlie Brown Christmas. Clifford the Big Red Dog.* A whole bunch of Shirley Temple movies. All the Bloom girls had at some point been obsessed with the little curly-haired actress. I still had a soft spot for *The Little Princess.* Poppy was now under Shirley's spell and was begging Mom and Dad for tap shoes. Luckily, they had not given in yet.

Finally, I found what I was looking for. I popped the movie into the DVD player and settled on the couch.

When I woke up the next morning on the couch, Mom

was standing in front of me, looking concerned. The TV screen was a mute blue, and Buster had abandoned me. "What's going on, Del?" Mom asked worriedly, pulling her bathrobe around her. "Are you stressed out? Do you have insomnia?"

I rubbed sleep from my eyes. "I've got it, Mom!" I explained. She looked at me, puzzled. "How to win back Olivia!" Mom sat down on the couch and I told her all about how Olivia and her fiancé had met. Then I turned the DVD back on, fast-forwarded to the right spot, and pressed play.

I explained my idea. Mom nodded, a big grin on her face. "I think this just might work!" she said. "I'll get on the Internet and do some research." She gave me a big hug. "I'll call Olivia right away. Del, you're a genius!"

Chapter Nine

Everything was perfect. The lights in the store were low-ered and candlelight flickered. The usually cluttered worktable and countertops were cleaned. We'd brought in a card table and covered it with sumptuous ivory linens. There were four place settings of Mom's best silver and china, even her great-grandmother's sparkling crystal. The centerpiece was filled with roses, hydrangeas, lily of the valley, and lilacs, with gorgeous sugared purple grapes hanging over the side, all artfully arranged by Mom. She had fussed over it for hours until it was perfect. Ivy spilled out, grazing the tablecloth. Crystal candlesticks, each with an ivory taper candle, surrounded the centerpiece.

I smiled as I set down a place card that read: *Olivia and Todd Worthington*, hand-calligraphed by Aster. One of her odd collection of talents, which also included speed-reading and crocheting.

The bell on the front door rang and the butterflies in my stomach dipped and fluttered like crazy. Olivia, her mother, and her wedding planner, Corinne, stepped inside. After leaving a dozen messages for Olivia telling her we had a new idea, Mom had been about to give up. But then, to our utter amazement, Corinne had called to schedule an appointment with us. And we had gone straight to work.

Olivia walked over to the table, her eyes glowing. Mom pulled out chairs and the three women sat at the table. That was my cue. I pressed PLAY on my iPod and the music began.

It was the soundtrack to the musical that had brought Olivia and her fiancé together — *The Sound of Music*. I walked up to Olivia and presented her with a headpiece. It wasn't just any headpiece. It was a hand-designed halo of small silvery white star-shaped flowers.

"Is it —" Olivia started to ask.

"It's edelweiss," I confirmed.

We had created a headpiece out of edelweiss, the flower that plays such an important part in the musical.

Olivia reached out her hands. I held my breath. Did she like it?

"How did you know . . . ?" Olivia asked. Mom held up a mirror, and Olivia placed the headpiece on her head, arranging the yards of fine silk ribbon.

"Oh!" said Mrs. Post, her eyes filling with tears. "It's perfect!"

"Simply lovely," said the wedding planner.

"I can't believe it," Olivia said. "Edelweiss!"

"Just an example of the one-of-a-kind service you get from Flowers on Fairfield," said Mom with a smile.

And then the song "Edelweiss" began to play. A huge grin spread across Olivia's face. She opened her purse, pulled out her cell phone, and dialed a number. "Listen to this," she said, then held the phone up. She put it back to her ear. "What do you think?" she asked giddily. "I know! Me too!" she exclaimed. "See you later, sweetheart."

She turned to us, beaming. "And now we have our wedding song!"

Olivia's mom looked uncertain. "'Edelweiss' as your wedding song? Isn't it the Austrian national anthem?"

The wedding planner blanched. "Well it's certainly . . . original!" she said.

Mom cleared her throat. "Actually, the Austrian national anthem is 'Land der Berge, Land am Strome,'" she said.

We all looked at her in surprise. *Nerd alert!* I thought.

She blushed. "I looked up *edelweiss* on Wikipedia," she explained.

"But is the song . . . appropriate?" Olivia's mom asked.

Mom smiled. "Any song that means so much to a couple is always appropriate," she replied thoughtfully.

This seemed to placate Mrs. Post. Olivia smiled at my mother gratefully. The wedding planner looked relieved and nodded enthusiastically.

I couldn't stand the suspense. "So is Flowers on Fairfield your wedding florist?" I asked.

Olivia nodded. "Of course!" she said.

Mom and I grinned at each other.

While Mom finalized the details with Olivia and her mom, presented the paperwork to be signed, and happily accepted a down payment, I took the headpiece from the reluctant bride. I wrapped it in pale pink tissue paper and nestled it into a box.

"So what changed your mind?" Mom asked Olivia when they were done. "The headpiece? The centerpiece? Seeing the table all set up? The music?"

Olivia and her mom exchanged a look. "Oh, I was always going with you guys," Olivia said hastily. She and her mom put on their jackets.

"Thank you!" cried Mrs. Post. "I know this will be a wedding to remember."

The door jingled shut behind them. Corinne lingered for a moment, looking as if she was deciding whether to say something or not. Finally, she spoke. "You didn't hear this from me," she said, "but Olivia was going to hire Fleur to do her flowers for the wedding. But then she ordered one of their virtual bouquets for her mom's birthday and she totally hated it. And there was just no time to go anywhere else!" She smiled at us. "See you soon!"

Mom and I frowned at each other as the door closed behind her. "That isn't exactly what I was expecting to hear," Mom said, biting her lip. "But we'll take their business . . ."

". . . any way we can get it!" I finished.

To celebrate our success, Mom invited Dad, Rose, Aster, and Poppy to the store.

"We won back our bride!" Mom announced, ushering everyone in. "Thanks to Del and her *Sound of Music* idea."

Dad admired the beautiful table setting. "You did a great job, girls," he said to us. He kissed me on the cheek and gave Mom a big hug, lifting her up in the air.

"Me next!" squealed Poppy.

"I love *The Sound of Music*," said Rose. "Someday I want to play Liesl," she said, and launched into a spirited rendition of "Sixteen Going on Seventeen." I bit my tongue to keep from reminding her that she was only ten going on eleven.

"So will the groom be wearing lederhosen?" Aster asked with a smirk.

"Very funny, Aster," I replied.

After we took apart the wedding display, Dad manned the phones, taking incoming orders. Mom made several birthday arrangements and a very blue "It's a Boy!" bouquet. But meanwhile, Poppy was running wild, and no one seemed to care. Rose and Aster said they wanted to help, but then they didn't seem too interested in the jobs I asked them to do, like break down boxes, throw away dead flowers, or dust the vases. We were low on cash-and-carry bouquets, so I was arranging roses, gerberas, and statice together, rubber-banding the stems, wrapping them in cellophane, and tying them up with ribbons. I liked to curl the ends for a festive look.

Rose decided her job was going to be to greet customers. "I will be the face of Flowers on Fairfield," she announced. She began to practice. "Welcome to Flowers on Fairfield," she said, tightening her ponytail and striking a pretty pose. Next she tried, "We welcome you to our fine floral establishment." Then, "Hello, ma'am/sir. May I interest you in some flowers?" And people seemed charmed by her — when she actually greeted them. But half the time, she didn't even notice when a customer walked in.

She was too busy clutching one of my cash-and-carry bouquets to her chest, looking in the mirror and practicing her Academy Award acceptance speech. Even worse, she always seemed to leave one person out in her litany of thank-yous — me.

Aster finally *did* take the dead flowers away — but then she created bouquets out of them. To my extreme annoyance, Mom took the biggest one and displayed it on the counter! She and Dad thought it was the cutest thing ever. Two dozen shriveled roses in a vase filled with plastic spiders left over from our Halloween display. Tied with a jaunty black ribbon. Aster looked very pleased with herself.

"That's not a good idea," I whispered to Mom. "What kind of florist displays dead flowers?"

"Oh, Del," my mom said. "It's funny." She tousled my hair. "Come on, honey. Lighten up."

Lighten up? My entire family needed to start taking things more seriously!

At school on Monday, I was walking down the hall on my way to English class. I was a little nervous because we had public speaking that day and I knew chances were I would have to present. That's what life is like with a last name like Bloom. Always at the mercy of the alphabet. You'd think, just for once, they'd start with the Zs. But no, straight to the beginning of the alphabet every time.

I spotted Heather turning away from her locker, about to merge into the crowd. I waved to her and she fell into step beside me.

"How are things going at the store?" she asked.

I sighed. "I'm being overwhelmed by Blooms!" I said.

She laughed. "That's a good one!"

I had to smile. I hadn't meant it that way, but it sounded like I was complaining about the amount of flowers we stocked. Then I sighed. I wished that were the problem!

Just then, someone stepped on the back of my sneaker and gave me a flat tire. If Heather hadn't grabbed my arm I surely would have wiped out. "Hey!" I said, annoyed, as I turned around.

It was Hamilton! "Hey!" he said, his face bright red. "Sorry, Del!"

I moved to the side of the hallway to pull my shoe back on. Heather and Hamilton joined me.

He frowned. "I'm so sorry. Hope I didn't hurt you!"

"I'll survive," I said.

Heather cleared her throat. "Del, aren't you going to introduce me to your friend?"

I gave her a withering glance. I knew what she was up to. "Hamilton, this is my friend Heather Hanson. Heather, this is Hamilton Baldwin."

"Hey, Heather," said Hamilton.

"Pleased to meet you," said Heather primly. "Are you new?" she asked as if she didn't already know.

"I am," said Hamilton.

"And are you enjoying all that Sarah Josepha Hale Middle School has to offer?" she asked with a bright smile.

I groaned.

"Why, yes I am," said Hamilton. "I've met some really cool people."

Just then the late bell rang. Students scattered.

"See ya!" said Hamilton, waving as he walked backward down the hall, and narrowly missing running into a boy in a baseball cap.

"He likes you!" hissed Heather just before she took off for class.

She left me sputtering in the hallway. "Wait — how . . ." But she was gone.

"Exhibit A," said Heather when I cornered her at her locker after school. Amy was there, too, so we lost valuable time as Heather quickly recapped the Flat Tire Episode. Not that I was desperate to know exactly how Heather knew he liked me or anything, but still. "He smiled at you when he said he had met some really nice people."

"Really?" I said. "Are you sure he was smiling at me and not just smiling?"

"Positive," said Heather.

"Exhibit B," she continued. "He backtracked down the hall after the bell rang." She nodded knowingly.

"Interesting," said Amy.

"Because that's where his class was," I said.

"Oh, Del, must I explain everything to you?" said Heather. "My goodness, you are dense sometimes." She shook her head, her history book in her hand, mid-shelve. "That means he had already passed his classroom. So the only reason he was still walking down the hall was to follow you."

"What if he was going to the water fountain?" I asked.

Heather shuddered. "Only losers drink from the water fountain, Del. I thought everyone knew that."

Amy nodded.

This was news to me. "Is there an exhibit C?" I asked.

She shelved her history book and turned to me. "Yes," she said seriously. "The most interesting one of all. You only give someone a flat tire if you are following behind them too closely." She cleared her throat. "Therefore, I must conclude that he was trying to listen to what we were saying!"

I shook my head. This was all too complicated for me.

Heather slammed her locker shut. "I know what I'm talking about, Del," she said. "Your crush boy likes you back."

Amy took off her glasses and polished them on her shirt. "I wasn't there," she said, holding them up to check for smudges, "but I'm convinced he likes you. If anyone knows crushes, it's Heather."

I didn't even try to argue. Mostly because I wasn't sure I wanted to.

❀   ❀   ❀

"Girls, I'm home!" Mom shouted when she walked in the door that night. "You're never going to believe what happened at the store today!"

Buster began to bark like a maniac. I put my mechanical pencil down on the kitchen table and stood up. I was looking for any excuse to take a break from my boring science homework. I strolled into the living room and joined my sisters, who'd been watching TV. Dad was working in his study.

"Olivia changed her color scheme again?" I guessed.

"Olivia wants me to be her flower girl!" crowed Poppy.

"Customers were asking why your beautiful daughter Rose wasn't there to greet them?" suggested Rose.

Mom turned to Aster. My sister shrugged. Mom grinned at her.

"No — we sold Aster's bouquet!"

Aster looked really surprised. But not as surprised as I felt.

Mom scratched Buster behind the ears as she explained. "A goth girl came in to send an arrangement to her aunt in the hospital. I did a very cheerful snapdragon and freesia piece — really sweet. While she was waiting, she saw the dead-roses-and-spider arrangement on the counter and fell in love with it for herself. She wants four more for her friends!"

"Wow," said Aster. She looked pleased — well, as pleased as Aster can look.

I opened my mouth, about to say something. *Florists sell live flowers! Not dead ones!* But Mom was giving me the hairy eyeball. She shook her head and the look was definitely *Del, keep your mouth shut.*

So I did. But I wasn't very happy about it. Earlier that day, after the public-speaking torment in English class, we had learned a new vocabulary word. The word was *disgruntled.* And it was exactly the way I was feeling about this whole flower shop situation.

Mom must have sensed this, because after I was already in bed that night, she came to my room and quietly stood in my doorway.

"Now, I don't want any arguments," she began softly. "But I'm going to need all hands on deck at the store this Saturday. It's the day before Mother's Day and there will be lots of orders and walk-in customers. Plus, next Saturday is Olivia's wedding. And the night before that is opening night of Rose's play. So we're going to have to finish everything early to make it there on time."

"But . . ." I started to say, thinking about how hectic it was when my sisters came to the store.

Mom held up her hand. "No buts. Everyone is pitching in. End of story."

"Fine," I said, and rolled over on my side, turning my back to my mom. She stood there for another moment, then closed the door.

I felt terrible. I knew I was being stubborn and *disgruntled*, but I couldn't help it. I had to do something about this crazy family of mine before they officially drove me insane.

Chapter Ten

The next day after school, Amy asked me to stay late to help her with Spanish homework. By the time we were done, the halls were pretty deserted. I knelt in front of my locker, loading up my backpack, when a pair of feet — a pair of very large feet to be precise — came to a stop in front of me. I stared at the worn-out green-and-black-checkerboard Vans.

"If it isn't Miss Dental Hygiene," said Hamilton.

I could feel myself blush, but fought down my nerves.

"Hey," I said nonchalantly. At least I hoped it sounded nonchalant. I stood up, slipping my bag over my shoulders. "How are you?"

"Fine," he said. "I've been meaning to ask you a question. Something I've been wondering." He paused. "Are you walking home?"

"I am," I said.

"Mind if I join you?" he asked.

I gulped. "Sure," I said.

He gave me a funny look.

"I mean, no. I don't mind," I said.

We took off down the hallway. I looked up at him. "So what were you wondering?" I asked.

"I was wondering if you knew the reason why Mr. Howard's clothes look so funny," he said.

As we headed out the door I laughed and explained that our history teacher's suits were five sizes too big — because he had lost a ton of weight but was too cheap to buy new clothes. Hamilton thanked me for clearing that up. Then he told me about the new alien movie he was dying to see, and I pretended to be somewhat interested. Suddenly, as we were coming up on Willow Street, he stopped and pointed.

"Hey," he said, sounding intrigued, "this looks like a nice park. Can we cut through it?"

I wanted to tell Hamilton that it was just a regular old playground, but since he was new, he must have found the regular old things in our town somewhat interesting. Which was kind of refreshing for me, too.

And that's how I found myself strolling through the

kiddie park on a blustery spring afternoon. All the toddlers must have been home drinking hot cocoa or watching *Yo Gabba Gabba!* or something, so we had the whole place to ourselves. When Hamilton suggested we sit on the swings, I said sure. When he started pumping his legs, I joined in. At first I felt ridiculous, but then I gave in to the joy of it, soaring back and forth, not a care in the world.

We swung in companionable silence until the sun started to set and our hands were chilled through by the metal chains. I pried mine free and rubbed them together for warmth as we left the park. And I was pleased to notice that Hamilton walked me all the way home.

"Cool house," he said, studying the widow's walk. "I bet it's great for hide-and-seek." And with a wave, he was gone.

I walked in the door with a big smile on my face, not even noticing the pile of toys and shoes in the front hall. Then my smile faded when Rose appeared in front of me, hands on her hips.

"Where were you?" she cried. "You promised you'd run through my *Bye Bye Birdie* lines with me. You promised!"

Oh no. I grabbed Rose's arm. "I'm really sorry; I totally forgot."

Rose's mouth fell open. "You totally forgot, huh? What kind of a sister are you?"

"Sorry, Rose," I said. "Um, can't we just do it right now?"

She scowled. "I already ran through them with Aster. Too late."

I really felt bad. "Is there something I can do to help?" I asked.

Rose brightened. "Actually, there *is* something you can do. You can ask Aunt Lily a favor for me."

"What?" Surely Rose was kidding. Ask mean old Aunt Lily for a favor?

"We're short on costumes and I need to get some nineteen fifties–style clothes for the show." She smiled. "Guess who was a teenager in the fifties and still has everything she ever wore stored up in her attic?"

"I guess that's where Aunt Lily comes in," I said with a sigh.

"Yes, and I'm afraid to call her. So I need you to do it."

I groaned. "Like *I'm* not afraid?" I said.

Rose gave me a little shove. "You? You're not afraid of anything!" she said.

While I was flattered that my little sister thought of me

that way, I was really shocked. I couldn't *not* think of things I was afraid of — big hairy spiders. Public speaking. Horror movies. Identical triplets. And, of course, Aunt Lily.

The last thing I wanted to do was call Aunt Lily. But I felt guilty about disappointing Rose again. And she was giving me those puppy dog eyes. "Okay," I finally said.

"Lillian Davis," said my great-aunt crisply when she answered the phone.

"Oh, hi, Aunt Lily," I said nervously. "This is Del. Del Bloom," I added unnecessarily. "How are you?"

"Fine, Delphinium," she answered. "And you?"

"Great," I said. "Um . . ."

"And to what do I owe the honor of a phone call?" she asked. "I can't remember the last time one of you girls called here."

"Well, I need to ask you a favor," I explained.

"Ah," said Aunt Lily. "A favor. And what might that be?"

I explained the situation. There was a long silence.

"I do have several boxes of old clothing," Aunt Lily said. "Including one from the fifties. Tell Rose that she should come to my house tomorrow evening at six o'clock to pick it up. Not five forty-five. Not six fifteen. Six o'clock on the dot."

I admired her precision. "Thanks, Aunt Lily. I will."

"And tell her if anything is ripped or stained she will be held responsible."

"Of course, Aunt Lily," I said. "Thank you."

"You are quite welcome," said Aunt Lily. Then she made a dry sound that might have been a laugh. "Imagine the day when the dungarees you are wearing today are used as props in an old-fashioned play, Delphinium. Imagine that."

I said good-bye, shaking my head. Nobody called jeans dungarees anymore. But still, she did have a point.

The next evening, Rose and Dad brought the box of clothes home. We all gathered in the living room as Rose started pulling clothing out. It was a treasure trove of cool fifties fashions — poodle skirts and sleeveless blouses. Neck scarves and pencil skirts. Aster tried on a beaded black cardigan sweater. Poppy covered herself in scarves. Rose pulled a pair of cute, shortish, pale blue pants on over her leggings. "These would be perfect for my first scene," she said excitedly.

"Cute!" said Mom. "I like those pedal pushers!"

"Petal pushers?" Poppy giggled. "Do you wear them to push flowers? That's funny!"

"Not petal," Mom corrected. "Pedal. They're pants you'd wear while riding a bicycle so your pants leg wouldn't get caught."

"I like it my way better," said Poppy stubbornly.

"I do, too, Poppy," said Mom.

I stared at the assortment of young, fun outfits. "I just can't picture Aunt Lily wearing these clothes. Was she ever really a teenager?" I said.

"Wait a minute!" cried Mom. She jumped up, ran to the bookcase, and pulled down a photo album with a tattered cover. She turned the pages until she came to one and stopped. "This is it!" she said. We all joined her at the coffee table, jostling around to get a good look. There was Gran, when she was must have been about ten years old, with the same halo of curly hair — except then it was blonde, not snow-white — and cheerful smile. And next to her stood a girl who looked a few years older, with wavy, long light brown hair and wide, hazel eyes, in a sleeveless blouse and a pair of pedal pushers.

"That's Aunt Lily," said Mom.

"Wow," I said. The girl was pretty. And happy-looking, too.

"She looks just like *you*, Del!" said Rose.

I took a closer look. I didn't want to admit it, but it was true. Even the way she was standing, her hands on her hips and her weight on one leg.

Just like *me*.

On Friday afternoon, I was still thinking about the picture of Aunt Lily. It was so weird how different she had looked — but how much I looked like the girl in the photo. On my way to math class, I ducked into a stall in the girls' bathroom on the first floor. While I was in there, I heard two girls walk into the bathroom, chatting. I instantly recognized the voices: Ashley's handmaidens, Sabrina and Rachel. I was about to open the door when I heard something that made me freeze in my tracks.

"So like Josh Gilson told Melissa Packer that that new guy Hamilton has a crush on someone!" Sabrina said.

I leaned forward in the stall, holding my breath. Who did he have a crush on? My heart started beating faster. *Could Heather have been right? Could it be . . .*

"Josh said it's a girl in Hamilton's gym class," she continued.

Gym class — that's me! I thought. *Or is it . . .*

"So it must be Ashley!" Rachel squealed. "I knew it! I can't wait to tell her!"

"No fair! I get to tell her! It's like, my gossip!" said Sabrina.

"Maybe we could text her together," said Rachel.

"Oooh, I like that. But from *my* phone," Sabrina declared.

I peered out the crack in the door and saw them putting on lip gloss and flipping their long, straight brown hair. I looked at my watch. The bell was about to ring. I was going to be late for class, but I couldn't let the handmaidens see me. Too embarrassing. So I waited.

"They would make the cutest couple ever, wouldn't they?" said Rachel, and Sabrina nodded, giggling.

Finally, they left. I waited a couple of seconds, then left the stall, washed my hands, and sprinted to class. But I was late, and had to do an extra-hard math problem on the board as a result. Talk about adding insult to injury!

❀   ❀   ❀

"Del, are you coming?" called my mother bright and early that Saturday morning. "We're heading over to the store!"

In my bedroom, I pulled my gray hoodie over my head and twisted my hair back in a sloppy bun. I had woken up in a bad mood. Could it have something to do with what I'd overheard in the bathroom yesterday? *Nah,* I thought. *That can't be it.*

I headed to the top of the stairs to see Mom, Dad, Rose, Aster, and Poppy zipping up their coats, ready to head out. Then I had an idea. I smiled. "I'll meet you all there!" I called down the stairs.

Let my family get the store ready this morning, I thought. While Mom and Dad opened the new shipments, Rose could haul out the buckets of flowers and display the premade bouquets. Aster could check the answering machine for orders that had come in while we were closed. Even Poppy could help, sweeping up or something. I needed some alone time. I'd go in later to help with the orders, once the place was ready.

Unfortunately, I just couldn't relax. I tried to read a book, but couldn't focus on the words. I couldn't even concentrate on a rerun of *Project Runway* on TV. I tried organizing my bookshelves, but as it turned out, they were already in perfect order. So, much sooner than I had expected, I was making my way to Flowers on Fairfield.

I stood in front of the door (it could use a good Windexing, I noticed), sighed, and pushed it open.

Ring-a-ling-ling! No one even looked up. They hadn't heard me come in because the radio was blaring. And what a mess! There were stacks of unopened boxes of flowers on the floor. Mom and Dad were nowhere to be found. Aster was making another one of her dead-flower arrangements. Poppy and Rose were dancing in the middle of the store. What if I had been a customer!

That's when I lost it. "What is going on here?" I cried.

No one heard me. I stomped over to the counter and shut off the music.

"This is a business!" I yelled. "Not our living room! When are you guys going to realize that?"

Poppy looked at me. Her chin trembled. And then she started to cry.

"Nice one, Del," said Rose, glaring at me. "Making your baby sister cry!"

Aster just shook her head and continued with her arrangement of death.

I took a shaky breath. I hadn't meant to yell. I looked at my sisters. "I'm sorry, Poppy," I began. "I didn't mean to . . ."

I glanced up and saw that Mom and Dad had appeared (paper cups of coffee in hand, so I knew where *they* had been) and were staring at me, looking concerned. Poppy ran over to Mom, who quickly put down her coffee and picked her up.

"Del scared me," Poppy said, sniffling. "She's mean!"

"Del," Mom said softly. She bit her lip. "Maybe it would be better if you went to Becky's for the day. We can handle things here."

I couldn't believe it. I was getting kicked out of the store. *My* store! I was suddenly mad again. "Fine!" I said. I turned around and stormed out the door.

"Have a nice day!" called Aster sarcastically.

Like I said, she doesn't talk much, but when she does, she makes every word count.

"Del!" said Becky, surprised. She opened the front door, still wearing her pajamas. "What are you doing here? Aren't you supposed to be at the store? Olivia's wedding is just a week away!"

I groaned. "No one wants me there," I said. "I kind of flipped out today. My sisters — and my parents — are making a mess of the place! They're ruining everything. It's so *frustrating*, Becky."

I followed her into the spotless living room and flopped down on her couch. "Watch out for the throw pillows," said Becky, removing one from under my butt. "My mom doesn't like anyone to sit on them."

"The store was my place. Mine! And now suddenly my sisters are everywhere. They're not even helpful. They just get in the way!" I hugged a round pillow to my chest. Becky gently removed it. "You are so lucky you're an only child," I added. "You don't have annoying sisters who try to take over your life."

Becky leaned forward, her brown eyes big and thoughtful. "Del, I think you're so lucky to have a big family," she said. "Everything seems like so much more fun with other people around. There's always someone to do stuff with."

"And always someone to fight with," I said bitterly.

"Yeah," she said like it was a good thing. There was a beat of silence. Becky chewed on a thumbnail nervously.

"Now, don't get mad at me, Del, but I feel like I need to tell you something."

"What?" I said warily.

"You'll still be my best friend no matter what I say?" she asked. "You won't get mad?"

"I promise," I said.

"I think you need to . . . lighten up a little bit. Just because your family isn't doing things exactly the way you want them to be done doesn't mean it's wrong."

I felt my face get warm. I'd lied. Now I was mad at Becky, too. Did *no one* understand me?

"Whatever," I said shortly. "I don't want to talk about this anymore."

"But . . ." Becky started.

I stood up. "I better go."

Becky looked upset. The two of us hardly ever fought, and I knew she expected me to apologize. But I was too *disgruntled* to be good company. I'd be better off alone.

Things were tense in my house. Aster spoke even less than usual. And whenever Rose started telling a story about the play, she clammed up when I walked into the room. Even little Poppy was giving me the cold shoulder. "I'm feeling angry, Del," she told me seriously. "That means I am not happy," she explained.

I couldn't argue with her there.

At dinner on Sunday night my sisters and I ignored Mom and Dad's attempts to get us to talk to one another. I went straight to my room afterward and shut the door.

When I brushed my teeth before bed, I could hear Rose and Aster in their room, practicing Rose's lines for the play. *Well, I blew that one*, I thought. I hadn't run through a single scene with her. Then I shrugged. Who cared, anyway? Not me!

But I *did* care. I hated being at odds with my family, annoying as they might be. I decided it was time to make a call. I needed advice from someone who understood the entire situation. Who knew how I felt about the store and what it meant to me. I promised myself that I would take whatever advice this person had to share.

"Delphinium!" boomed Gramps. "We just got back from the sunset at Mallory Square. It was so much fun! There are all these performers — fire-eaters and musicians. A guy was making balloon animals! And there was a man who blew bubbles and played music while his dog collected money in her mouth! While wearing boxers! And then the sun set and we all applauded! It was great!"

"The dog collects money while wearing boxers?" I asked, giggling. My grandparents were certainly embracing the Key West life with open arms. "Sounds great, Gramps." I could hear my grandmother in the background. "What did Gran say?" I asked.

"She says she thinks she saw that flash of green when the sun went down that everyone talks about." He lowered his voice. "But I think she's making it up!"

"Tell Gran I miss her," I said, feeling a little choked up.

"I will," he said. "So what's going on, Del? You sound down."

So I filled him in. I told him everything. That the store wasn't being run properly and my sisters were making a mess. About the dancing. The petals on the floor. The dead flower arrangements. And the complete disregard for the way things should be done.

There was silence after I finished. "Gramps?" I said.

"I was afraid of this," he finally answered. "You got too used to having the store to yourself. And I guess that's our fault."

"But Gramps," I protested. "They do things all wrong!"

"The flower shop is a family business and your sisters have every right to help out, too," he said gently. "And it's okay that they don't do things the same way we did. It reminds me of when your mom first started working in the store when she was in high school. She drove Aunt Lily crazy with all her ideas."

"So what happened?" I asked.

"Your aunt drove her crazy right back, criticizing everything she did. Your mom finally quit and went to work at the ice-cream shop." He sighed. "I've always regretted not intervening. Just because someone does things differently doesn't mean they're wrong."

I was disappointed. And I was officially tired of being compared to Aunt Lily. But maybe Gramps had a point. *Maybe.*

"And here's another thing. Even though your mom might not be running the store the way you like, I bet you anything she's been doing some really nice arrangements."

I thought about the bouquet with the strawberries. The "Happy Birthday" arrangement with the multicolored candles. Mom really *was* creative.

"She has," I admitted. "Oh, I don't know, Gramps, it's just so hard without you and Gran here." Then I brightened. "Well, at least you'll be home in two months," I said. "Right?"

"Yeah, about that . . ." Gramps started to say. Then he changed the subject. "So how are the Movie Nights going?" he asked.

"Um, they're not," I admitted. "It just didn't feel right. I like things the way they used to be."

Gramps sighed. "You're a little young to be so set in your ways, Del."

We said our good-byes and then I sat in my room, thinking. Maybe Gramps was right. Maybe there was more than one way to do things. After all, it's not like I was perfect, or even close. I had done some dumb things in the past couple of weeks. I had shot down my family's ideas just because they were different. I had been judgmental and selfish. I had wanted the store all to myself, but that wasn't a possibility anymore.

I hated to admit it, but maybe it was time to make some changes.

The question was — *how?*

Chapter Eleven

The first person I wanted to set things right with was Becky. On Monday morning, I waited for her at her locker.

"Hi there," she said, dropping her backpack to the floor and peeling off her jacket. She sounded a little aloof, and I could understand why.

I plunged right in. "I'm sorry I was such a jerk at your house this weekend," I said, looking her right in the eye. "I hope you're not too mad at me."

She laughed. "You're my best friend, Del. I can't stay mad at you for long. I know things have been hard with the flower store."

I was so relieved. I gave her a big hug and then we went to the cafeteria, where I bought her a hot chocolate. With extra whipped cream.

Making up with my sisters was not going to be so easy. I had to come up with a plan.

It took me all week to figure it out, but I finally did, and right in time, too.

It was the day before the wedding, and the opening night of Rose's play. I skipped out of school after second-to-last period. Mom had written a note to get me out of gym class so I could head to the store early and help her and Dad assemble the centerpieces and bouquets. I wasn't sad to miss gym, even though, thankfully, we'd stopped our square-dance lessons and had moved on to basketball. But Ashley was still talking to Hamilton all the time. And I'd see more than enough of Ashley on Saturday at the wedding.

I met my parents at the store and we worked steadily, creating piece after piece. As the sun started to set, I glanced up at the clock — one hour to curtain! Mom was putting the finishing touches on Olivia's bouquet.

She yawned. "Almost done — can you believe it? We'll actually make it to the play on time!"

I went into the back room with some flowers, ribbon, and cellophane. I had some making up to do with my sisters. And I was going to say it with flowers.

I stashed the bouquets under my seat and looked around the auditorium. I waved to my friend Jessica, who sat a couple of rows behind us with her parents. Her brother was in the fourth grade and in the chorus. She waved back and made the "call me" sign, her hand to her ear. I nodded and smiled. Then I glanced over at Aster. She deliberately hadn't sat next to me and that made me feel bad. She looked paler than usual. She always gets nervous before Rose's plays. Rose says that she never gets butterflies because Aster does it for her. Dad patted Aster's hand reassuringly. On my other side, Mom folded up her coat for Poppy to sit on. The orchestra began to play and the curtain rose. Showtime!

It turned out that *Bye Bye Birdie* is a really funny play, with catchy songs that had most of the audience dancing in their seats, my family included. Of course, we all paid closest attention whenever Rose was onstage. Rose was really convincing as a starstruck teenager. At one point

Mom leaned over me to whisper to Dad, "I can see what's ahead for us!"

Rose also looked very cute in Aunt Lily's blue pedal pushers, which, with Aunt Lily's permission, of course, she'd had tailored at the dry cleaners so that they fit perfectly.

I was really proud of my sister, but felt bad that I hadn't helped her with the lines. Next play, for sure. I kept reaching under my seat to make sure that the shopping bag of flowers was still there.

After the curtain calls (two!), we pushed our way backstage with the other beaming families. Rose was surrounded by cast members, all congratulating her.

"Everyone ready to go to Oscar's for dinner?" asked Dad after he and Mom had hugged and complimented Rose.

We all nodded excitedly. "Do they have hot dogs at Oscar's?" asked Poppy. We all laughed.

"I can't wait to see how my arrangements look!" said Mom. I couldn't wait to get to Oscar's, either, but for a different reason. I was planning to present the flowers to my sisters during dinner. I'd make a short, heartfelt speech, Mom (and possibly Dad) would cry, and we'd all make up.

We arrived at the restaurant at 7:00 on the dot. We hadn't been to Oscar's in a long time — not since Mom and Dad's anniversary dinner last year — and I'd forgotten how fancy it was: full of flickering candles and tables covered in crisp white cloths. I always feel kind of self-conscious in such formal places. I clutched my paper bag to my chest as Aster, Rose, Poppy, and Mom gabbed excitedly about the play. Meanwhile, Dad told the hostess, "We have a reservation for seven o'clock. The name is Bloom."

"We'll seat you in a moment," said the hostess.

Just then a waiter walked by, carrying a large arrangement of flowers.

"Hey!" said Mom. "I made that!"

"And it's beautiful," said the hostess. She lowered her voice. "But we had to remove it. You see, there's going to be a rehearsal dinner in our banquet room at eight o'clock tonight. The mayor's son is getting married tomorrow," she added. "And it turns out that the mayor is deathly allergic to lilacs!"

It took a minute for her words to sink in.

Then I pictured fifty carefully arranged centerpieces of hydrangeas, roses, ivy, lily of the valley, and *lilacs*.

"Olivia knows that there are lilacs in the centerpieces," I said slowly. "She would have told us!"

"Maybe she doesn't know he's allergic!" Mom exclaimed, looking panicked. "And you know how Olivia is — she got so wrapped up in what *she* wanted for the wedding . . ."

"It could have slipped her mind," I filled in, my worry growing.

"This is bad, right?" Aster spoke up, and Mom nodded.

"Uh, we need to cancel our reservation," Dad told the hostess. "Family emergency!"

The worktable at the store was littered with piles of lilacs, half-eaten half-sour pickles, cans of Dr. Brown's soda, and the remnants of our hot-dog dinner. Not exactly the gourmet feast we had been anticipating, but delicious just the same. Luckily, the local deli was good, and it delivered.

In between eating and the lilac removal, we had a lot of fun. At first I was going to say something about waiting to enjoy ourselves until after we were done fixing the flowers, but I kept my mouth shut. And I was glad I did. Mom cranked up the music and we took turns dancing. Then Rose suggested a game of charades and we guessed movie titles.

I suppose you can *mix fun with work,* I thought, laughing as I watched Dad try to act out my suggestion, chosen for its humor potential and level of difficulty: *Die Hard 2: Die Harder.*

This would have been one boring evening if my family hadn't been there to join in. And the best part was that my sisters were all in good moods and were actually talking to me again.

But I knew I still needed to say something to them. I turned off the music and cleared my throat.

"Speech! Speech!" called Dad.

I nodded at him. "I just wanted to apologize to you all," I began, feeling a little nervous. I cleared my throat. "I've been a jerk."

"Here, here!" said Aster, toasting me with a Cel-Ray. Rose laughed and clinked cans with her. Who in their right mind drinks Cel-Ray? That's *celery* soda. Yuck. I made a face at both of them.

"Well," I continued. "I'm sorry. I know I haven't been very good at sharing this place with any of you. But I also know that Gran and Gramps left it with all of us, and that we all have a right to be a part of Flowers on Fairfield. And actually, we all *need* to be a part of it. Tonight proves that. We all need to work together to make this place a success."

Mom spoke up. "I've been thinking, too, Del," she said. "And if you girls are in agreement," she added, looking at my sisters, "I think it would be great if Del taught you all she knows about the store and how things work."

"Really?" I said, feeling hopeful.

Mom smiled. "Really," she answered. "You just have to be open to other ways of doing things."

I looked at Rose, Aster, and Poppy. "Are you guys okay with that?" I asked them.

Aster nodded. Rose dramatically threw her arms around my neck and kissed my cheek. And Poppy wrapped her arms around my legs in a sticky hug — her hands were very mustardy, but I didn't even mind that she got some on my skirt.

"Wait, I almost forgot something!" I cried. I ran over to the shopping bag I had been carting all over town. I reached in and pulled out the first bouquet.

"Rose," I began. "You were truly a star tonight and I am really proud of you. I made an arrangement of some very special roses — called Broadway Blooms. Because this Bloom is going to star on Broadway someday."

Rose took the bouquet and inhaled. "They smell amazing!" she said. "And look, they're yellow and pink — my favorite colors!"

"I think you are going to be the best greeter the store has ever seen. You're so friendly and so good with the customers."

Rose blushed. "Thank you, Del," she said.

I reached into the bag and pulled out a slightly squashed bouquet of big red flowers. "Poppies for my little sister Poppy," I said. Poppy let out a squeal of delight. "Poppy, I promise to be more patient with you from now on," I said solemnly. "And I will come up with fun things for us to do around the store together."

"That sounds good, Del," said Poppy, clutching her flowers. "And now I feel very happy."

"And for you, Aster . . ." I reached into the bag one last time.

"Let me guess," she said with a grin.

I shook my head. "I promise to listen to your ideas. In fact, I think you should start a line of goth flowers. There are plenty of cool, *live* flowers you can use," I said, handing her the arrangement. "Black hollyhocks," I told her. "Note that they are tied with black ribbon."

"They're amazing," she said.

I looked at my sisters. "I've missed you guys."

"Well, you'll be seeing plenty of us now!" Rose said.

"My girls are friends again!" said Mom, wiping her eyes with the black bandanna she uses for special occasions.

Dad, always the goofball, stood up and wrapped his arms around all four of us in a huge hug. "Daddy! My poppies!" Poppy cried.

He let go of us with a grin. "'After a good dinner'," he quoted, pointing to the deli remnants, "'one can forgive anybody, even one's own relations'!" He paused. "Oscar Wilde."

As we began cleaning up, I had a thought. I grabbed an assortment of flowers, floral tape, and ribbon.

"What are you doing?" Mom asked, holding an armful of lilacs.

"Better safe than sorry," I said. "I'm going to make one more bridesmaid's bouquet."

Rose yawned. "You're crazy."

"It does seem unnecessary, Del," said my mom. Then she saw the serious look on my face.

"If there's one thing I learned tonight," I said, "it's to expect the unexpected."

Mom grinned. "You do have a point there!"

Everyone cleaned up around me and left me to work.

It didn't take me long, but I was exhausted by the time I finished wrapping bright pink ribbon around the stems of my bouquet. I looked around. The place was clean, and Mom had finished replacing the very last centerpiece in the cooler. Poppy lay curled in the corner, sleeping on a pile of coats. It was late, we were tired, but we were done.

"Time to go home," said Mom.

We drove back to the house, and Dad carried the still-sleeping Poppy up the stairs to her room. "See you tomorrow, bright and early," he said.

I looked down at my watch. Yikes! Mere hours till the mother of all weddings. I needed to fall asleep, and fast!

Chapter Twelve

I woke up the next morning, my stomach already in knots. It felt like I'd barely slept. Probably because I hadn't.

Tired as I'd been the night before, I had laid out my clothes before climbing into bed. I decided in honor of the wedding to go completely girly — a purple empire-waisted dress with teeny pink flowers, pink tights, and my cute but comfortable black Mary Janes for all the running around I knew I was going to do.

I yawned a jaw-cracking yawn on my way to the shower. We had a crazy day ahead of us.

After breakfast, Poppy led me upstairs to her room, where her pink party dress hung on the doorknob.

"I want to wear this dress just in case," she said.

"Just in case of what?" I wasn't sure what she was talking about.

Poppy rolled her eyes. "Del! In case Olivia needs a flower girl!"

"Oh," I said. I knew she was going to be disappointed, but there was no time to argue with her. "Okay."

"One more thing," she said. "I want you to have this for luck." She reached into her bathrobe pocket and stuck something small and plastic and fuzzy into my hand. It was a tiny troll doll with bright blue hair and a blue jewel in his — or was it her? — belly button.

I was touched. "Thank you, Poppy," I said. I tucked the troll into my dress pocket and helped her get changed.

Once everyone was ready, we gathered on the porch as Mom locked the front door behind us. I smiled. Olivia had lucked out. It was a cool morning, but the sky was clear, not a cloud in sight.

We went straight to the store, where I did a last-minute bouquet count, Rose tallied up the corsages and boutonnieres, and Aster counted the centerpieces. All set. I checked for any wilted blooms, but everything looked as fresh as it had the night before. Dad started loading up the centerpieces into the delivery van.

Our plan was this: Mom would drop me off at Olivia's house with the bouquets for her and the bridesmaids, and the corsages for her mom and grandmother. Then Mom and my sisters would head to the church with the rest of the corsages, the boutonnieres, pew decorations, and altar flowers. Once I was done at Olivia's, I would meet Mom and my sisters at the church. After the wedding, we would go to the Country Club where Dad would be. We'd help him finish decorating and then go home to relax for a while before heading out to the second night of Rose's play. Whew!

"Whoa!" Mom said as we pulled up the circular driveway in front of Olivia's house.

Whoa was right. The house was huge. Maybe even a mansion. It had tall columns and a wide lawn. Plus, those bushes that are trimmed into funny swirly shapes that look like soft-serve ice-cream cones.

"Good luck," said Mom as I climbed out of the car. "Call if you need anything. See you at the church!"

Rose and Aster helped me get the big box of bouquets and corsages out of the back and carry them to the front steps. I waved good-bye to them as I stood on the marble front steps and rang the doorbell. No answer. The door was unlocked, so I stepped inside. I could hear voices upstairs, so I walked up the large staircase, carefully balancing the box of flowers in my arms.

"Hello?" I called when I got to the landing.

A bridesmaid, her hair set in large rollers, poked her head out of a doorway. "The flowers are here!" she cried. Bedroom doors began to open and I saw bridesmaids, in various stages of bridesmaid dress. Some were getting their makeup done, others were having their hair styled. I went from room to room handing out bouquets to everyone. They all smiled happily and thanked me. "They're gorgeous!" said one of the bridesmaids, taking a deep sniff. "Simply gorgeous!"

In the last room, there was Ashley, sitting at a mirror and looking pouty while the other bridesmaids got ready around her. I approached my nemesis nervously. I had resolved not to be anything but completely professional today, but I was sure that wasn't going to be easy. I handed her the bouquet and she took it from me without a word.

"Looking good, Ashley," I said.

"Go away, Delphinium," she replied, turning back to the mirror to reapply lip gloss to her already well-slicked mouth. Maybe she was in a bad mood because she didn't get to wear the sleek navy blue bridesmaid dress she had been bragging about, but instead was clad in the junior bridesmaid version — which had a very full skirt and goofy puffy sleeves.

"Has anyone seen the flower girl?" I asked.

One of the bridesmaids grimaced and pointed to a room down the hall. As I got closer, I could hear the shrieks. I knocked on the door. A harried-looking woman in a black sheath dress answered. Behind her, I could see a little girl on the floor in full temper-tantrum mode in her pretty pink flower-girl dress.

I smiled. "Here's the flower girl's basket!" I said cheerfully.

The girl's mom rolled her eyes and shook her head. "Meltdown," she said. "She stayed up too late at the rehearsal dinner. I'm sure she'll settle down in time for the ceremony."

"Good luck!" I replied. *You'll need it!* I thought. I was glad Poppy was past the temper-tantrum stage.

Just then the maid of honor reappeared and escorted me to a large bedroom — and there was Olivia, sitting in front of a dressing table. I gasped. Her blonde hair was in a sleek French twist and the delicate headpiece we had made for her looked like a fairy crown. She stood up and her dress rustled around her. It was a strapless cream-colored silk gown with beading on the top. The skirt was full, draped delicately in gathers that looked like ripples in the water. Olivia was always pretty, but today she looked breathtakingly beautiful.

"You . . . you . . . you look like an enchanted princess!" I said.

"Oh, Del," said Olivia. "Thank you!"

I handed her the bouquet, a simple arrangement of creamy white roses and cascading ivy. "It's just perfect," she told me, cradling it in her arms. Corinne, the wedding planner, who'd been fussing with Olivia's train, nodded her approval.

Olivia's mom and grandmother were in the room, too, so I handed them their corsages. The photographer was there and started snapping away as Olivia pinned the flowers on their dresses.

"One more thing," I said. "Your ring bearer's boutonniere."

"Where is he?" asked Olivia.

"I haven't seen him in a while," her mother said worriedly.

The maid of honor left the room and reappeared, carrying the ring bearer, clad in a tiny black tuxedo. He whined and twisted his head around and tried to bite the collar. Did I mention that the ring bearer was named Louis Vuitton? He barked at me as I fastened his boutonniere. He didn't like it one bit.

Finally, my work there was done. I walked down the large staircase, placed the extra bouquet in a box by the front door, and stepped outside. As I closed the door behind me, I heard a clip-clopping sound. *That's weird,* I thought. *It sounds like a horse.* And sure enough, a horse and carriage pulled up in front of the house. The bridesmaids all spilled out of the house, laughing and chattering away. The photographer was right behind them.

"While we're waiting for the bride to come downstairs, let's take some photos of you girls with the carriage!" suggested the photographer. The bridesmaids laughed as they clustered around the big white horse. The redheaded bridesmaid reached up to stroke his velvety nose.

Just then the horse, who apparently had not had his breakfast that morning, leaned over and took a big bite out of her bouquet. Maybe it was the strawberries that got his interest.

"Help! Help!" she cried. She yanked on the bouquet and ended up with a handful of slobbery half-eaten flowers. She looked like she was going to cry.

The horse, on the other hand, looked very pleased with himself. The photographer snapped a quick succession of photos of the horse, a bright pink rose hanging out of his mouth like a cigar.

"Where is the wedding planner?" cried the maid of honor. "We have an emergency!"

"Nothing to worry about," I told her. I ran inside, reached into the box, and pulled out the extra bouquet. *Just wait till I tell my family,* I thought proudly.

Soon, Olivia came out of the house, waving to her bridesmaids like she was royalty. But I couldn't be annoyed at her — it *was* her special day. Everyone cheered. The photographer began positioning her and her bridesmaids in front of the swirly-looking bushes. I checked my watch. It was about half an hour till wedding time, so I decided to head over to the church. I waved good-bye to everyone and walked the ten blocks in a quick trot.

From down the block I could see guests streaming into the church. I wove through the crowd, climbed the stairs, and walked through the big wooden doors. I stood in the vestibule, watching the tuxedoed ushers showing people to their seats — bride's side on the left, groom's side on the right.

I smiled. My family had done an amazing job. The church looked so beautiful it could have been on a movie set. Sunlight streamed through the stained-glass windows, leaving pools of rainbow light on the marble floor. Long swathes of white tulle ran down the center aisles, wrapped with ivy. Small nosegays of white and pink roses hung from each pew. The pink, purple, and off-white displays on the altar were big, but natural looking. Mom had somehow made them look like the world's largest handpicked bouquets.

Someone placed a hand on my shoulder. I turned around. It was Mom. Aster and Rose stood beside her.

"What do you think?" Mom asked. She looked a little stressed.

"It's perfect," I assured her.

She smiled at me nervously. "I can't believe it," she said. "It's really happening!"

"I know," I said. "All that hard work and here we are!"

She took a deep breath. "Okay, Aster, Rose, and I are going to get the runner ready," said Mom, referring to the white fabric that would go down the aisle for the wedding party to walk on. "Are you okay back here with Corinne just in case anything goes wrong?"

"Fine," I said. "But where's Poppy?"

Aster pointed to the corner of the vestibule.

Rose shrugged. "She's waiting for Olivia, just in case she needs her."

"Poor Poppy," I said. "She's going to be so disappointed."

I found my littlest sister standing in the corner by one of the side doors, looking serious.

"Poppy," I said gently. "I already gave the flower girl her basket of rose petals. So you're probably not going to be able to walk down the aisle today."

Poppy stuck out her lower lip. "Maybe she'll need me," she said.

I sighed. Talk about stubborn!

Maybe I wasn't the only one who'd inherited that trait from Aunt Lily.

I heard the clop-clopping of horse hooves and poked my head outside. Olivia, her dad, and Louis Vuitton had arrived, Louis looking dashing in his little doggie tux as he sat on Olivia's ivory lap. Three limos full of bridesmaids were there, too. The guests were all seated. The groom and the minister were waiting by the altar. It was almost time to begin.

The bridesmaids began to file inside and fill the vestibule, whispering to one another excitedly. Corinne arranged them in order, giving last-minute instructions. The runner was rolled out. The music began and a hush fell over the guests. The first bridesmaid gave a nervous grin over her shoulder and set off down the aisle. I did a quick head count. Someone was missing. Where was the flower girl?

"No! No! No!" I heard a child shrieking.

I ran to the front door. The flower girl's mom was

trying to drag her up the church steps and the little girl was pitching a fit. "I want to go home!" she hollered.

Corinne was right behind me. She grabbed my arm, a panicked look in her eyes. "What are we going to do?" she asked.

I turned to the little girl's mother. "Do you think she'll do it?" I asked.

"I'm afraid she'll scream the whole way down the aisle if I force her," she said with a sigh. "But I hate to disappoint Olivia."

"I've got it covered," I told her. "Don't worry. I just need to borrow your daughter's headpiece and basket."

The woman gratefully handed everything over.

I walked back inside to where Poppy stood in the corner. I had a big grin on my face. I couldn't believe this was actually happening. "You still want to be a flower girl?" I asked her.

Her eyes lit up. "Really?"

I placed the headpiece on her head and adjusted it. I handed her the basket. Her eyes were shining with excitement.

"Now you go down the aisle right after the junior

bridesmaid, and right in front of the maid of honor," I told her. "You need to walk with the dog *and* drop the petals on the way. And then you sit down in front. On the left. That's *this* hand."

She nodded solemnly. "On the left," she repeated, holding out the correct hand. Then she beamed at me. "I'm going to be a flower girl!" she said. "I knew it!"

While Corinne did some last-minute adjusting of Olivia's train, I took Poppy's hand and led her to her place in line. I found the maid of honor. But where was Ashley? I asked one of the bridesmaids if she had seen her.

"She said she went to check her lip gloss," she told me distractedly. *Uh-oh.* It was nearly time for Ashley to go down the aisle. Where was she?

As I was looking around, I spotted the maid of honor holding Louis Vuitton.

"Oh, great! I need the ring bearer," I said to her.

"Here," she said happily, handing him over. I placed the little dog on the floor, next to Poppy. He looked up at me, walked over to a pillar, and raised his leg.

"Louis Vuitton!" I cried. I raced forward, scooped him up, and took him outside. That was a close one!

I came back inside just in time to see Ashley come sauntering back. The bridesmaid in front of her had just taken off down the aisle. "It's almost your turn!" I said.

"Calm down, Delphinium," she said coldly. "I'm fine. I was just in the bathroom."

She stood in the doorway, tossing back her hair. Poppy stood behind her, her mouth open in a little "o" of surprise.

Because Ashley's puffy skirt was firmly tucked into the back of her underwear.

Ashley Edwards, my arch-nemesis, was about to completely humiliate herself in front of hundreds of her family members, friends, and neighbors!

Poppy looked at me. I paused for a long moment. And then, with a sigh, I reached over and gave her skirt a yank, pulling it back into place. My dreams of Ashley's complete and total humiliation were dashed before they even began. It would have been the perfect YouTube moment.

"What are you doing?" Ashley yelped. Then her eyes widened. "You mean I almost . . ."

I nodded silently.

She gulped. But before she could say anything, it was her turn to go down the aisle. Ashley nearly stumbled as she set off. I watched her go, smiling. I knew I had done the right thing, tempting though it had been not to.

I sent Poppy down the aisle next, Louis Vuitton at her side, and a huge grin on her face. I watched her as she scattered the flowers just as if she had been practicing for weeks. Which she had. She made it to the end, scooped up Louis, and sat down next to Ashley. The maid of honor was next. I breathed a sigh of relief before I headed over to Olivia to see how she was doing.

She was clutching her father's arm nervously as Corinne adjusted her veil.

"Everything's fine," I said reassuringly. "You look beautiful."

"I know I forgot something," she said.

"What could you have . . ."

Her eyes flew open. "Something old, something new, something borrowed. Oh no, I forgot something blue!" she wailed.

She looked at her dad. "Do you have anything blue on you?" she asked in a panicky voice. He shook his head.

She grabbed Corinne's arm. "Blue? Do you have anything blue?"

The wedding planner reached into her purse and pulled out a blue Bic pen.

"I can't carry a *pen!*" Olivia said.

If only I had something blue! I thought. And then I remembered. I reached into my pocket and pulled out — the blue-haired troll doll.

"I know this isn't what you had in mind," I told Olivia. "But we can put it into your bouquet for good luck."

Olivia looked skeptical at first, but when I tucked the little creature into her bouquet, only a tiny bit of bright blue hair showed. She laughed. "Actually, it's kind of cute," she said.

The organist began playing "Here Comes the Bride." The guests all stood and pivoted to face the back of the church. I could see Olivia's handsome husband-to-be at the end of the aisle, smiling nervously.

Her father squeezed her hand reassuringly. "Olivia, my dear," he said. "It's time."

Olivia smiled and they took off down the aisle. I sighed with relief. Corinne and I gave each other tired smiles. This wedding business was stressful!

❀ ❀ ❀

Mom rushed up to me after the ceremony.

"I almost died when Poppy came down the aisle!" she said.

"Yeah," said Aster. "I thought she mugged the flower girl!"

Lucky Poppy got to ride in one of the limos with the rest of the wedding party. But Mom, Aster, Rose, and I piled into the car to go to the Country Club. When we arrived, we saw the guests heading into the part of the club that was hosting the cocktail hour. But we went straight into the ballroom, looking for Dad.

He grinned and waved from across the dance floor. "Doesn't it look great?" he asked, gesturing around the huge room.

And it did. The ivory linens cascaded to the floor. The silver, china, and crystal sparkled. The centerpieces were tall and elegant, yet fun and cheerful with all the pinks and purples and reds and the glistening sugar-coated purple grapes. The lights were dimmed and candles were ready to be lit by the waitstaff before the guests arrived. We helped with some last-minute adjustments to the centerpieces in the ballroom, but there really wasn't much left to do. I watched as the band set up and did a sound check. "One, two, three . . ."

"Hey, where's Poppy?" Dad asked.

"She left in a limo," said Mom with a laugh. "Maybe we should go find her!"

Uh-oh. "She must still be with the wedding party," I said. I could only imagine what my little sister could be up to. I rushed to the cocktail hour, where people were sipping champagne from delicate flutes and balancing small plates in their hands as they chatted with one another. I looked around in amazement. There was a sushi station, a man in a tall paper hat carving up big hunks of delicious-smelling meats, huge piles of crab claws, lobster tails, and more shrimp than I had ever seen in my life. I spotted an ice sculpture of the bride and groom's entwined initials. But I couldn't find one small substitute flower girl anywhere.

"Where is the bridal party?" I asked a man in an expensive-looking suit with a pencil-thin mustache. He told me they were in the greenhouse taking pictures. Sure enough, when I made it out to the greenhouse, there was Poppy, front and center, grinning away for the camera.

I looked at Corinne. She shrugged. "Olivia said she wanted the flower girl to be a part of the pictures!"

When the photographer was done, I took a still-grinning Poppy by the hand. The cocktail hour was over and the guests began filing inside the ballroom. I joined my family in the hallway just outside the doors and we watched everyone parade by in their wedding finery.

"There's the mayor!" whispered Dad. I looked over; his tuxedo shirt looked a little snug, but he was laughing and looked very happy. And not, thankfully, having a deathly allergic reaction to lilacs!

As the bridesmaids and groomsmen lined up in the hallway outside the ballroom, waiting for the bandleader to call their names, Olivia left her new husband's side and headed over to us. She gave each of us a hug and a kiss. "I couldn't have asked for a more beautiful wedding," she said. "You Blooms really outdid yourselves." She turned to Ashley, who stood nearby. "Don't you think so?"

"Yes," Ashley said sweetly. While Mom and Olivia chatted, she turned to me, her face serious. "You saved me back there."

"I know," I said lightly. "It would have been totally awk," I couldn't help adding.

She nodded. "Def." She smiled. "You guys did a really great job." She took a deep breath. "You know, at first I was happy when that wedding planner suggested that Olivia go to that other florist. But now I'm really glad you guys did it."

"Huh?" I said. Then it hit me — Ashley had had nothing to do with us almost losing Olivia's wedding! And I had been blaming her the whole time. I gave her a grateful smile. Maybe she wasn't as bad as I had —

Then Ashley spoke again. "But don't think I'll be nice to you at school because of this," she added snippily.

"I wouldn't dream of it," I retorted.

Just then the wedding planner rushed up to Olivia and whispered in her ear. "That's a great idea!" Olivia said, then turned to us, a smile on her face. "Turns out an entire table full of Todd's cousins are fogged in in DC and weren't able to make it. Would you guys like to come to the reception?"

"Yes!" shouted Poppy. We all laughed.

"But Rose's show tonight . . ." Mom said.

"We have plenty of time," Rose insisted, her eyes glowing.

Mom smiled. "Sure," she said, "we'd love to."

And that was how we ended up as guests at the wedding of the year. We were seated just in time to see Olivia and Todd make their entrance.

"Introducing, for the first time as husband and wife, Mr. and Mrs. Todd Worthington!" announced the bandleader. The crowd cheered. Then their song began to play for their first dance. "Edelweiss." I grinned, and Mom squeezed my hand.

Then I realized — all that hard work, all the craziness, was all for this moment. The beautiful bride and the handsome groom, dancing together. I got choked up as I saw Todd gently wipe a tear off Olivia's cheek. (Mom, of course, was wiping her face with her matching bandanna!) They were so happy together — and so much in love. Suddenly, I found myself thinking of Hamilton. A deep blush spread over my face.

Then the food started coming. Course after course of delicious food. My glass of ginger ale was never empty. Our work was done, so my family and I just relaxed and enjoyed ourselves. We laughed at the best man's funny speech. We gasped as an overenthusiastic bridesmaid tripped and slid across the floor in a mad attempt to catch the bouquet. We oohed and ahhed over the chocolate fountain with strawberries and pound cake for dipping. We danced and danced between courses. And then, at the end, we all got teary as the wedding party serenaded the couple with "So Long, Farewell," the good-bye song from the play that had brought them together, *The Sound of Music*.

And just before *we* left, my family took a moment to raise our glasses.

"To the Blooms," said Mom. "And the best family business in town!"

We clinked glasses and grinned at one another. We had pulled off the impossible — a demanding bride, a crazy schedule, and a whole lot of unexpected competition. And we had done it together.

When we got home late that night, after Rose's play, we discovered that the message light on our answering machine was blinking.

"Now who could that be?" Mom wondered aloud as she pressed PLAY.

"Hello!" Aunt Lily's voice rang through the room. "Congratulations! I heard you did a wonderful job at the wedding. I am very proud of all of you." Slightly shocked, we all grinned at one another again. But then she added: "You do realize that prom season starts in two weeks? Just a reminder! Have a good night."

The smiles left our faces. I could feel my heart sink. What was one bride compared to a hundred girls in fancy dresses?

No one said a word. Then Aster broke the silence with a low whistle. "Holy corsages!" she said, and we all burst out laughing. Poppy, who'd been fast asleep in Dad's arms, woke with a start, and miraculously started laughing, too.

I smiled at my family. My often crazy, sometimes annoying, and always there-for-one-another family. Together, we would figure this next challenge out.

"You said it, sister!" I replied.

Chapter Thirteen

We were all gathered in front of the computer screen, elbowing one another to make sure we were in sight of the video camera. It was our very first iChat with Gran and Gramps.

Suddenly, they appeared on the screen. "Oh!" said Mom. "There they are!" Seeing their familiar faces after all these weeks filled me with instant joy.

"Oh, it's so lovely to see you all!" Gran said. "Lily told us the wedding was a smashing success!"

"Yes, congratulations!" said Gramps.

"And how was Rose's play?" Gran wanted to know.

"It was great!" Rose said eagerly. "I'll send you the DVD really soon!" As she jabbered on about the show, I studied Gran and Gramps. They looked so tan and healthy. Gran had a big pair of sunglasses perched on top of her head and Gramps was wearing a very bright Hawaiian shirt.

"We wanted to talk to you in person." Gramps laughed. "Or as close to in person as possible. We have some news."

I took a deep breath. I had a feeling about what was coming next.

"We've made a decision," said Gran slowly. "We can't handle another New Hampshire winter. We love it down here so much . . ." Her voice trailed off.

"You're not coming back," I said.

Everyone looked at me, silent. "And that's okay," I went on. "You guys deserve to have fun. We can handle the store — as long as we do it together."

Everyone smiled at me. Poppy even patted my hand.

Dad nodded. "And now we have a great place to visit!"

Mom swallowed, then spoke. "I have a suggestion," she said. "It has to do with the store's name. Customers have been saying that Flowers on Fairfield sounds so old-fashioned." She bit her lip. "I know it's been in the family for years but I wonder if we could . . ." Her voice trailed off.

"Change the name!" boomed Gramps. "It's your store now; name it whatever you want!"

"I never really liked it, anyway," Gran confessed. "It *is* a mouthful!"

We started tossing names around.

"Flower Power!" said Rose.

"Bloodflowers!" said Aster. We all gave her a funny look. "It's the name of a Cure album," she said with a shrug.

"Blossoms?" suggested Mom.

"Blooms?" offered Dad.

"How about . . . something with Petals in it?" I asked, thinking of the rose petals Poppy had tossed onto the aisle at the wedding.

"I know, I know!" shouted Poppy. "Petal Pushers!"

We all were silent for a moment as we considered it. Then we all grinned. "That's it!" Mom said. "Great idea, Poppy!"

We said our good-byes to Gran and Gramps. It was a bittersweet moment. It was exciting to have the store all to ourselves. But it would be hard with Gran and Gramps so far away. Everyone looked so sad. I had an idea.

"You know how I feel about continuing with our Friday Movie Nights," I said.

"Yes," Dad said warily.

"But how about *Sunday* Movie Nights instead?" I said. "We can start tonight! We can eat an early dinner and watch a movie. It can be a new Bloom tradition!"

"It *is* a nice way to start out the week," said Mom.

"I like it!" Dad added.

"I love it!" said Rose, and even Aster beamed.

"I vote for cake batter ice cream!" said Poppy.

"No, peanut butter brickle!" Aster and Rose said together.

Mom and I were chosen to go out and pick up the supplies. We stopped off at the video store first. My friend Amy had told me about this funny old movie called *Galaxy Quest*, so I found it and handed it to Mom. She got in line.

I was checking out the new releases when I bumped into someone. I looked up. Yikes! It was Hamilton!

"Hey, Del!" he said. He held a DVD in his hands, but he angled it so I couldn't see the cover.

"Movie Night at your house, too?" I asked.

He nodded.

"Hamilton!" called a voice. "Did you find *My Big Fat Greek Wedding*?"

Hamilton blushed. "It's my mom's turn to choose," he explained.

I turned around — and there was a tall blonde lady waving to us from across the store. I squinted at her. She looked so familiar . . . And then I suddenly realized who it was. The lady from Fleur!

"Hey, how do you . . ." I started to say.

"Just a minute, Mom!" Hamilton called back.

Mom? I thought, bewildered. Then it hit me: Hamilton's mom was the owner of our rival flower shop! So *that* was how he knew that delphinium was a flower.

I was speechless. Could it really be?

Hamilton's mom started heading over to us. Luckily, my mother had just paid for our movie and came over.

"We're all set," she said, smiling at Hamilton.

"Great," I said. I grabbed Mom's arm and dragged her toward the door. "See you on Monday!" I called to Hamilton.

When we were safely out the door Mom said, "What was that all about?" She grinned at me. "And who was that cute boy?"

"It's a long story," I said, feeling dazed. "I'll tell you about it sometime, I promise." My stomach rumbled. "Let's make it quick at the grocery store. I'm starving." Then I had a scary thought. "Just promise me that *you're* cooking tonight!"

Mom laughed. "I promise!"

Turn the page for a
sneak peek at the next
Petal Pushers book
Flower Feud!

"May I ask how many prom orders you've gotten so far?" Aunt Lily asked.

"We were just discussing that," said Mom. "Not so many. But Del just told us there's to be a middle school prom, too, so we're feeling optimistic. . . ."

Aunt Lily cut her off. "As I suspected," she said. "It seems as if our rivals are trying to take away our business. Again."

"What do you mean?" I asked. My heart sank. I knew this couldn't be good.

"Benjamin, would you please hold up the paper?" commanded Aunt Lily.

Dad complied, lifting the paper so we had a full view of the front and back pages. And what we saw made us gasp.

The entire back page of Saturday's paper was an ad. An ad for Fleur. There was a photo of a girl's wrist with a simple orchid corsage on it. Under the photo were the words:

FLEUR.

ELEGANT. SOPHISTICATED. STYLISH.

WHY GO ANYWHERE ELSE FOR YOUR PROM FLOWERS?

Fleur is our competition. The new, fancy florist in town with software so you can design virtual bouquets. Fleur is in the mall, is twice as big as Petal Pushers, and has tons of flowers we don't normally carry.

And there's one more part of the Fleur story. The store is owned by Hamilton Baldwin's mom. Yes, Hamilton Baldwin — the new guy in school who I think is cute. The guy in gym class who Ashley has a crush on. But Hamilton doesn't know I know his mother owns Fleur.

As if things weren't complicated enough.

Mom took a closer look at the ad. "Oh my," she said in a small voice. "It says 'Become a Fleur Fan on Facebook'!"

So Fleur was at it again. Last month they had tried to steal away our first big job — a large wedding. Luckily, we had managed to keep it. Now they were taking out newspaper ads and creating Facebook pages. I glanced around our store. It was sweet, small, and very old-fashioned. We had no website, no virtual bouquets, and certainly no Facebook page.

"So you think everyone is going to Fleur instead of us?" Dad asked with a frown, putting down the paper.

"Yes," said Aunt Lily. "Especially if they're doing a lot of advertising."

Mom cleared her throat. "I'm sure all the kids will start coming in this weekend."

"I am, too," said Dad optimistically. "I'll bet we have a line out the door this very afternoon!"

"I hope you're right," Aunt Lily said. But she didn't look convinced. I didn't feel convinced, either. "Good day," she said. She gave us a curt nod and marched out the door.

We all stared at one another after she left.

"Well I think that proms sound bee-you-tee-ful," Poppy pronounced. "Mommy, can you make me a corsage?"

"Another time, my love," said Mom. "I have to start another arrangement. Del, can you help me?"

I busied myself cutting flowers for the new arrangement. But inside I was fuming. I couldn't believe Fleur was trying to take away our prom business.

This means war! I thought.

Catherine R. Daly has been a children's book editor for many years and has also written or adapted more than one hundred books for children. She lives in New York City with her family. Her middle name is Rose, which perhaps helps explain her lifelong love of flowers. Petal Pushers is her first series for young readers.